Just Like Ice Cream

Lissa Halls Johnson

TYNDALE

Tyndale House Publishers, Inc.
Wheaton, Illinois

JUST LIKE ICE CREAM

Copyright © 1982, 1995, 2005 by Lissa Halls Johnson
All rights reserved. International copyright secured.

Library of Congress Cataloging-in-Publication Data
Johnson, Lissa Halls, 1955-
Just like ice cream / Lissa Halls Johnson.
    p. cm.
"A Focus on the Family book."
    Summary: When her summer romance results in pregnancy, 16-year-old Julie receives support from her friend, a youth minister's wife, as she makes a life-changing decision—to have an abortion, keep her baby, or give it up for adoption.
  ISBN 1-58997-195-7
[Pregnancy—Fiction. 2. Sex—Fiction. 3. Decision-making—Fiction. 4. Conversion—Fiction. 5. Christian life—Fiction.] I. Focus on the Family (Organization) II. Title.
PZ7.J6325Ju 2005
[Fic]—dc22   2004013429

A Focus on the Family book published by Tyndale House Publishers, Wheaton, Illinois.

Focus on the Family books are available at special quantity discounts when purchased in bulk by corporations, organizations, churches, or groups. Special imprints, messages, and excerpts can be produced to meet your needs. For more information, contact: Focus on the Family, 8605 Explorer Drive, Colorado Springs, CO 80920; or phone (800) 932-9123.

Cover design and photography: Sally Leatherman

Printed in the United States of America
05 06 07 08 09 10/10 9 8 7 6 5 4 3 2 1

For Lee Roddy

Who taught me, loved me, believed in me,
prayed for me—
and who regularly hit me upside my
frizzy little head with a 2x4.

Thanks, Uncle George!

Chapter One

The radio crackled and fizzed. I leaned over the stack of unfolded clothes, adjusting the tuner.

The vibrant, sure voice of the DJ throbbed in my small room. "KBAY wings you back to the peak of the heat to bring you this former number one hit tune. So put on your summer gear and dream of the lazy days gone by."

> *You are my fantasy,*
> *My life, my love.*
> *I'll never leave you*
> *For another, another.*
> *I'll never leave you, my love.*

I couldn't believe it. I never thought I'd hear this song again. Suddenly I forgot about the pile of laundry that Mom had asked me to fold.

I sat there, biting my bent finger to prevent uncontrollable sobs. Soon the tears were running in torrents down my face.

The song spoke of love and hope. To me it meant lies, hurt . . . irreversible pain and loss.

> *You are the one forever and today.*
> *You are the one for always.*
> *I'll never leave you,*
> *I love you and I care.*

I'll never leave you,
I'll always be there.

"Oh, Kyle, you—liar!"

I wanted to scream, but the sound stuck in my throat. Instead, I let the song sweep me back to the time before Kyle. The time before the pain.

Too much had been lost. Innocence, love. Even a life. So much that I could never gain back.

I knew lots of girls would do it over again if they had the chance. But me? No. No way.

———————

The heat warmed our backs to an almost unbearable temperature. I turned to walk backwards as I spoke to Stephanie. "I wonder if Carol had her baby yet?" My tongue caught a drip from my ice cream cone at the last second.

Stephanie gaped at me. "What do you care?"

"I dunno. Just curious, I guess."

"Guess I'm curious, too." Stephanie tossed her head, shaking her golden hair away from her sticky cone. "I do feel kind of sorry for her."

"So why don't you talk to her?" I urged. Stephanie constantly tried to get me to talk to Carol at school. We had an ongoing argument about the whole thing.

"I said I feel sorry for her," Stephanie snapped back. "I didn't say I wanted to be buddies or anything." Then she looked thoughtful again. "She's nuts to keep her baby. No more fun, no more dates. Just baby all the time."

"Oh, come on, Steph, babies are adorable," I teased. "You can take them with you everywhere."

Stephanie's eyebrows rose. "Even on a date?"

I laughed. "With the right guy anything is possible, don'tcha think?" I raised my eyebrow, but she wouldn't bite.

"You'll never find me with a puffer belly like that," Stephanie said, using her favorite term for pregnant.

"Me neither," I agreed, adapting to her serious tone. "I mean, I want to have a baby—someday. Like in at least 10 years."

Stephanie looked at her watch. "Gotta run, Julie. I'm going to be late for work."

As she ran to her bike, I waved. My last summer without a job. My last summer of freedom. My last summer of being a bum. And I planned to make the most of it.

Turning to walk down the hill to the park, I thought about my friendship with Stephanie. She was my closest friend ever. Through fights and fun we'd always stuck together. We understood each other so well, we didn't need explanations about our behavior. I doubted there could ever be anything so awful that it could separate us. My dad always shook his head over our constant connection. "The gruesome twosome," he called us.

Comparing myself to Steph wasn't difficult. She had everything I lacked. She was gorgeous. If her blonde hair and perfect body weren't enough to catch the attention of every male in a one-block radius, her personality would. Even now, if I looked back to watch her pedaling to work, I would see cars slowing down as they passed and male heads turning to look.

I suppose I'm not too bad looking. People tell me all the time that I'm cute. But it's hard to believe them. I'd always thought Stephanie's blonde, curly hair was far prettier than my solemn, straight, brown strands. And I didn't think my body had caught up with my age. Maybe it never would.

Sighing deeply, I sat down in the grass. I thought at 16 your body was supposed to have fancy curves to it. Nothing fancy about my curves.

The warm sun shifted my thoughts to a better world, one where I could be whoever I wanted and look as great as I wanted. I kicked back and closed my eyes.

A low whistle soon pierced my daydream. Slowly opening my eyes, I looked up to see crystal blue eyes and a grin wide enough to be on any toothpaste commercial. Embarrassed, I reverted to my feel-at-ease tactic. Teasing. "Haven't I seen you on TV?"

"Not yet, hot stuff," he teased back.

"Why do you call me hot stuff?" I asked. "You can't know if the salsa is hot until you taste it."

Oops. My sassy self hadn't meant to be bold, only sassy. I cringed inside.

The grin grew wider. "OK, *possible* hot stuff, how about a taste? Meet you here Wednesday at six?"

Overwhelmed by the total *him*, I accepted.

I shielded my eyes to watch him pedal away when I realized we hadn't even exchanged names. I had to look away quickly when the sun reflected from a car bumper next to him, temporarily blinding me like a camera flash. Forcing myself up off the grass, I walked home in a daze. Sighing, I could still see that tanned body, with muscles in all the right places.

I chuckled, wondering how I'd noticed those flawless proportions after his sparkling blue eyes had held mine without wavering.

I jumped the two stairs to our porch and popped inside the house. "Hi, Mom," I chirped. She winced as the door slammed.

"Must you—"

"Mom, can I go out night after tomorrow?"

She looked up from the sink. "Don't you baby-sit for Jan?"

"No, that's Tuesday." When I stole a carrot she had just peeled, she made a move to slap my hand.

Turning back to her peeling and tucking a wisp

of hair behind her ear, she said, "I suppose it's okay.
. . . Now get busy and set the table."

As I unstacked the dishes, I thought how lucky
it was that she hadn't asked who I was going out
with. She would think it pretty tacky for her precious
little girl to go on a date with a nameless somebody.

Tuesday.

I thought about him all day. Not romantically,
though. I just let my mind ponder the possibilities
of who he could be and where he came from.

That evening I went to Jan's, and her 18-month-
old boy, Stevie, took my mind off him at least for a
while.

I never tire of baby-sitting Stevie. Maybe it's
because I enjoy his mother and father so much. Jan
and Rick are probably the greatest people I've ever
met. They make me feel so comfortable. I can be
myself around them and not be afraid they will look
at me weird if I say or do anything off-the-wall.

I love the way they tease each other with love
shining in their eyes. It all sounds so gushy to tell
it, but they really do love each other a lot. Their
only fault is sometimes they talk about God. I usually just ignore it. I suppose that's because Rick does
something at his church with high school kids.
Youth pastor, I think. I guess talking about God is
something they have to do.

Jan had been a cool friend for a year and a half now, so I knew I could tell her all about my date. She laughed when I told her I didn't even know the name of the guy I would be going out with.

⁕

Wednesday morning I let myself float into wakefulness. What a yummy feeling. I looked at the clock. Nine. Counting the hours until six, I decided what I needed to accomplish before then. Bolting upright, I cried out in horror. "Oh no! What if he doesn't show up? Maybe he talked to me just to take up air space. To be nice."

"Jule, are you talking to me?" Mom called.

"No, Mom." I turned and plunked back down on my stomach. Now what should I do? After thinking over all the options I decided to go, just in case. I peeled myself off the bed, gathered my stuff, and ambled down the hallway to take a shower.

That afternoon, walking to the park at five-forty-five, I kept checking my reflection in the store windows. I pretended to be browsing, though—I wouldn't want anyone to think I'm stuck on myself. My new white lace top created the perfect one-inch gap above my jeans, showing off my tan. I anticipated his look of appreciation.

If he's there.

As I walked down the final hill to the park, a sharp *slap, slap, slap* occupied my attention. The noise of my flip-flops was bouncing off the building walls and echoing back at me.

Then I heard that mellow voice drifting up to me. "Hey, possible hot stuff. I hope those flip-flops are bringing you in this direction."

I looked down the hill to see a very handsome figure lying under a tree. "They're on voice command," I called in return. "I programmed them to your voice."

"Is that all I am to you?" The grin was back. "Just a voice?"

Approaching him, I stuck my hands in the back pockets of my jeans, returning the smile. "That's all you are until I get a name out of you."

"If a name will help, it's Kyle. Kyle Browning. And what, may I ask, is yours, possible hot stuff?"

Putting my hands on my hips, I tilted my head to one side. "I don't know if I should tell you."

He lay back, hands behind his head, and closed his eyes. "Makes no difference to me," he droned. "I'll just make up my own name for you."

"And what might that be?"

"Oh . . ." He looked at me through one squinting eye. "Something that suits you . . ." He closed his eye. "Bozo, maybe."

I kicked his foot. "Julie suits me better than Bozo."

The eye opened again, this time coupled with

a raised eyebrow. "Oh, I don't know about that." The grin came back in full force as he sat back up, crossing his legs. He began to pull and toss individual blades of grass. "Julie what?"

I plopped down beside him. "Not Julie What. Julie Marshall."

"Hello, Julie Marshall," he said, sticking out his right hand. "Glad to meet you. Was that proper enough?"

I answered with an ugly look.

He jumped up, grabbing my hand in the process and pulling me up, too. He let go as soon as I stood. As I brushed off the seat of my jeans, he said, "How does a sandwich sound?"

"I don't know." I smirked. "I've never listened to one."

Shaking his head, Kyle asked, "Hot stuff, are you hungry for a sandwich?"

I tossed my head back and laughed. "Sure."

On the way to the deli we talked about all the usual stuff. About my dad being in construction, his in real estate. About my older brother, Matt, and younger sister, Tammy. His lack of any siblings. About the fact that he lived in my town during the summer and in San Francisco, or "The City" as we called it, during the school year.

My heart dropped a couple notches when I heard that. Living in The City meant there would be no long-term relationship with me. I filed the information away and continued the discussion, which had now progressed to family pets.

It seemed the only things we accomplished during dinner were filling our stomachs and laughing a lot. We finally decided it was time to remove ourselves from the deli before someone else did it for us.

The rest of the evening we spent walking all over town. I could say we talked, but that would almost be a lie since we spent most of the time laughing.

I did learn he loved music, and he discovered my favorite love is ice cream.

Although we didn't talk much, I felt I really knew him when he walked me to my door. He surprised but pleased me when he didn't try to kiss me goodnight. I'm shy about kissing on the first time out. Then the thought slid through my brain, *Maybe he didn't enjoy himself.*

"See you tomorrow," he said, his voice quiet.

"Bye," I answered as he loped off the porch and lifted his hand in response. I wondered if I *would* see him again.

"Oh, I hope so," I said into the darkness. "I really hope so."

Chapter Two

Thursday morning. Pure pittsville.

I woke feeling overwhelming dread. Some nagging intuition told me I'd never hear from Kyle again. That I must have done something stupid, said something stupid. I didn't have any rational reasons to think this. But it sat as leaden truth in my heart.

I waited until Mom left for work before dragging my body out of bed. I didn't want all the usual light talk about how my date went. I knew I would answer, "It went all right . . . right out the door."

After my shower, I poured some Cheerios into a plastic mug and sat down to watch the morning game shows. I thought about calling Stephanie as I'd promised, but didn't know what to tell her either.

As I munched the Cheerios, all I could think about was Kyle and analyze every moment and every word to see if I could have done something to make him never want to see me again.

The phone rang. I froze. At the third ring, I grabbed it. "Hello?"

"What's the deal?" a familiar voice teased.

My voice shook a little. "What do you mean?"

"I'm down here at the park, and the one I'm here to see is either invisible or not present."

"And who might that person be?" I asked, my teasing kicking into gear.

"You, my little nut."

I couldn't speak. I knew if I did, I would say something stupid. He had been out *looking for me!*

"Well?"

"W-well, what?" I stammered.

"Well, are you coming to the park or not?"

"Give me an hour." I hoped he wouldn't change his mind.

Kyle became so silent I knew he must have decided against seeing me. "An *hour?* Okay. Instead, meet me at that ice cream place on the corner."

Relief filled my voice. "Kramer's? Okay."

I hung up the phone, then pushed autodial for Steph. I told her all about Kyle while choosing my best kick-around clothes and dressing in record time.

Flying out the front door, all I could think of was the joy of seeing Kyle again. He'd kept his word. I was going to see him today!

I tried walking slowly to Kramer's, a futile attempt to hide my excitement. Kyle pushed the door open from the inside. "What took you so long?" he asked.

I looked at my watch. "Only one hour and five minutes. What's your rush?"

Kyle hesitated and seemed uneasy for the first time since I had met him. "I just hoped to see you before I left for The City today."

My heart dropped. He was going back.

"It's only for one night. I'll be back tomorrow. Can we go to a movie when I get back?"

"Not unless it's on DVD. I have to baby-sit."

"Can't you cancel?" Kyle was almost pleading.

"Sorry. It's for Jan." I sounded like I needed to go to a funeral. "She depends on me. I promised last week." For once I wished I wasn't so loyal.

"Who's Jan?"

"She's a friend." I waited until the waitress served our sandwiches before continuing. "Why don't you come over there? They leave at six. Stevie goes to bed at seven. So if you come at seven-thirty—"

"I'll be there," Kyle broke in.

I drew him a map on my napkin. He looked at it and nodded. He stuffed it into his pocket, then looked at me and flashed his grin. Popping the last bite of sandwich into his mouth, he said quickly, "See you, Julie. Tomorrow at seven-thirty." As he stood up, he leaned over and kissed me on the cheek.

I never even saw him ride away on his bike— or Stephanie arrive on hers.

Chewing my sandwich, I looked up to see her rushing to my table smiling from ear to ear. "Who's the hunk?" she asked.

I paused, then gave her a coy smile. "Kyle."

Disbelief registered on her face. "*That's* Kyle?"

"Yep," I said, trying to act indifferent.

We continued discussing Kyle through our sandwiches, ice cream, shopping . . . all the way until Stephanie had to go to work.

At home, it was easy to tell Mom what Kyle and I had done the night before, now that I knew he might be around for a little while.

Friday dragged on until I thought I couldn't wait another minute to see Kyle.

I didn't tell Jan that Kyle would be coming over. That was a first. I always tell Jan everything. But I couldn't risk her saying no. I *had* to see him that night.

After I put Stevie to bed, I checked the clock every two minutes. I sat in one chair, then another. I picked up every magazine, bouncing my foot as I flipped through the pages without seeing them. I must have looked at myself in the mirror 20 times before the doorbell rang.

"Come in," I said, sounding like a butler.

Kyle didn't look nervous at all. He stepped through the door in the calm, casual, self-confident way he seemed to do everything.

"Have a good trip?" I asked, closing the door.

"Of course not," he said with a smile. He took off his jacket and draped it over a chair.

Sitting on the edge of the couch I asked, "Why not?"

"It wasn't any fun without you." He slipped his arm around me as he sat down. "I missed you."

"I missed you, too," I said in mouse volume. Afraid to look at his face, I looked at his foot where it rested on his knee.

Kyle took hold of my chin and turned my face to his. "Did you really?"

I nodded my head.

His kiss was soft and gentle. So unlike anyone else I had ever kissed before. I thought I would melt right into the couch. The kiss ended and I thought I would die before I got another.

Backing away, Kyle looked into my eyes. "I knew it!"

"What?" I asked, afraid he didn't like my kiss.

Kyle kissed me again and said, "I gave you the right nickname—hot stuff. I'm a good judge of things like that."

I just smiled, and he kissed me again.

At the end of the soft kiss, he stood and went to his jacket. He slipped his hand into a pocket and withdrew a CD.

"Julie, while I was gone I heard a new song I thought you might enjoy, so I bought you the CD."

"Thanks!" I said. Taking the CD, I tore off the cellophane and headed for Jan's sound system. "Which song is it?" I called over my shoulder.

" 'I'll Never Leave You.' Third song."

I popped the CD in and tapped to song three.

You are my fantasy,
My life, my love.

I clasped my hands together and turned to look at Kyle. My eyes questioned the meaning of the words.

I'll never leave you
For another, another.
I'll never leave you, my love.

The song continued, and Kyle's smile drew me across the room. I cuddled up to him and put my head on his shoulder.

You are the one forever and today.
You are the one for always.
I'll never leave you,
I love you and I care.
I'll never leave you,
I'll always be there.

When the melody finished, I turned to Kyle and kissed him. "Thanks," I said, looking right into his eyes.

"I guess that was worth spending my money on."

"Thanks a lot!" I said, giving him a playful punch on his arm.

The rest of the evening we cuddled and watched

a romantic comedy from Jan's DVD stash. Every once in a while we'd pause the movie to talk or kiss. (I liked the kissing best.) When the movie ended, Kyle pointed at the kiss which ended the story. "I don't believe it," he said.

"That they're in love?"

"No. That they spent all that time together and never had sex."

"Oh, come on," I said. "It was sweet. They weren't sure where their relationship stood until the end."

"I still don't believe it." He took my chin and gave it a quick kiss. "Most people I know have sex after a few dates."

I shook my head. "Sad, isn't it? I think it's great when two people wait until they really care for each other."

"So you've never—"

I shook my head. "I'm waiting for the right guy and the right time."

"When would that be?" he asked, his gentle eyes boring into mine.

I shrugged. "Probably when I'm in college. But if I'm super-dedicated to my studies, I might be 25 before that happens. You?"

Kyle raised one eyebrow. "I dunno," was all he said before he kissed me again.

I hated for the night to end. I had never felt so loved and cared for in my life. My parents didn't often show much love or affection to me—or to each other, for that matter. I missed that affection I saw in other families. I longed for hugs, for touch, for a kiss on the top of my head. But my family just didn't touch each other. Besides, even if they had, this was different. Here was someone who thought I was special. Someone who didn't have to think so.

When we parted, I reluctantly let go of his hand with the promise that we would meet at the park in the morning.

Days began to fly by. Every day overflowed with thoughts of Kyle or with time spent with him. I had no time for anything else. Every moment began and ended with Kyle.

We rode bikes and horses. We went water skiing with friends. We hiked and picnicked and played.

Over and over I listened to the CD he'd given me, always taking special notice of "our" song.

Stephanie began to fade out of my life. The only time I saw her was when Kyle and I were getting ice cream at Kramer's. She always had a new guy in tow and seemed more distant each time. I didn't really care. If she didn't understand that we could still be friends . . .

It felt like more than three weeks since Kyle and I had first met in the park. But that's how long it had been when the sweltering day arrived that began to change my whole life.

On that day my craving for an ice cream cone consumed me more than usual. Lying on my bed, I felt desperate for one. I counted my change and didn't even have enough for a single scoop.

When the phone rang, I flopped my arm over my head and grabbed the cordless. "Hello?"

"Hi, hot stuff, how about a double scoop today?"

"Ummm. Sounds perfect," I said, my voice husky.

"Meet me at Kramer's?"

"You bet!" I said, sitting up and chasing away the heat-induced laziness.

"Okay, I'll give ya 10."

I ran a brush through my hair, but something kept bugging me. I frowned, thinking. I tapped the brush against my palm. *What is it?*

Something in Kyle's voice had sounded different. *Smoother than usual? Hungry?*

Maybe.

I tried to ignore the little thing that ate at me, figuring my intuition was messing with me again.

I finished brushing my hair, and dropped the brush into the drawer.

"See ya, Mom," I yelled as I skipped the bottom three steps. "Ice cream with Kyle."

"Bye, Jule. Glad to see you've got him so well trained."

"Oh, *Mother.*"

I could hear Mom yelling after me as I ran out the door. "If you aren't careful you'll get fat from too many ice cream cones."

I just shook my head. *Moms are so weird.*

Kyle must have called from Kramer's, because when I got there he held a half-eaten cone in one hand and a whole but melting strawberry cone in the other. Strawberry! My favorite. I caught him licking around the edge of *my* strawberry cone.

"Hey, you. I think your tongue is attracted to the wrong cone," I said.

"How do you know it's yours, hot stuff?"

"Why, it's got my name right on it." I grabbed the cone before he could eat any more of that precious stuff.

We walked away from the shop. The ice cream seemed to fill my veins, giving me some relief from the heat.

Kyle watched me eat my cone, and he smiled. "You love ice cream, don't you, Julie?"

"It's the best," I agreed.

"What if you never had any ice cream until you were 25? Say your parents protected you and felt it wasn't good for you. Say you finally had some and found out you loved it like you do now. Wouldn't you be disappointed that you hadn't started enjoying it sooner in life?"

"Well, yeah," I answered, a little confused.

Kyle paused, then took a deep breath. "Okay, my little hot stuff, I want you to try something just as good as ice cream. Something everyone regrets they didn't start enjoying sooner. Are you game?"

I smiled, feeling a bit impish. "Sure. What is it?"

Kyle winked. "Come with me and I'll show you."

A weird silence captured us as we walked through town, finishing off our cones. We rounded a corner and Kyle began to climb the steps to his house. I held back, feeling strange.

"Coming?" His eyes pleaded as his eyebrows rose.

"Give me a hint," I said.

"Just come on," he said, grabbing my hand and taking me up with him. We laughed as I tried to guess what this new experience could be.

"If it's caviar, you can forget it. I don't care if it is a delicacy. I'm not eating any fish eggs."

"It's not caviar, nut."

"If it's beer, you're too late. I had my first and last experience when I was 14. It makes me sick."

Kyle just laughed.

"Hey," I said as the door opened into a quiet house. "Where's your mom?" I liked his mom a lot.

She was friendly without being in our faces all the time. It was obvious from the way she dressed and talked that Kyle's family had plenty of money, though, and I felt a little intimidated around her.

"She and Dad went to The City for the week. He had business; she had a wedding shower to attend."

"Oh, who's getting married?"

"Not important." His answer was curt as he pushed the door closed with his foot. Now his hands and arms were full of me. He had never kissed me with so much passion before.

I squirmed away. "Okay," I said, my heart racing. "Where's my new experience?"

He hesitated. He took a step back. He spread his arms and flashed a crooked grin. "Well, hot stuff . . . it's me."

"What do you mean, you?" I asked, hoping he didn't mean what I thought he did.

He tilted his head to one side, gathered me back into his arms, and said, "All of me."

"But, Kyle . . ." My protest sounded feeble.

"Remember. It's just like ice cream."

I looked down at the floor. The idea scared me. But at the same time it appealed to me.

It wasn't as if I'd never thought about sex before. I thought about it all the time. Steph and I giggled late into the night many times talking about what it might be like. And who it would be with. We'd been to slumber parties where someone had smuggled R-rated movies. Who could be alive today and *not* think about sex?

So why not Kyle? I knew we cared so much for each other. And I did love ice cream. I certainly would have kicked myself had I kept from trying ice cream until I was older. Was sex the same as ice cream? Would I love sex as much as ice cream?

Kyle sprinkled soft, tender droplets of kisses on my ear and neck. I began to melt.

Once won't hurt, I told myself. *What's the purpose in waiting, anyway?*

What if you get a disease?

I could feel myself rolling my eyes at my own thought. *You can only get a disease if you fool around with a lot of people. Or from someone who fools around. We don't.*

The negative voice persisted.

What if you get pregnant?

Something else inside me scoffed. *No one gets pregnant the first time.*

I allowed myself to return his kisses just as passionately as he gave them.

It didn't take long for us to get our clothes off and climb into bed. I was surprised my nakedness didn't embarrass me. Maybe because he enjoyed it so much. And it all felt so nice. My whole body seemed to crave what he offered.

But then . . . it hurt. No one had told me the

first time might hurt. I wanted to cry out, but instead bit my lip.

When he finished, he kissed me once on the cheek, rolled over, and went to sleep. I felt like I wanted to cry. But I couldn't.

It wasn't that I was sad. Just ashamed. Also amazed. *That's it?* I thought, disappointed. *That's what everyone is talking about as marvelous?*

I got out of the bed in slow motion so I wouldn't wake Kyle. I felt funny as I walked to get my clothes. Suddenly I had to run to the bathroom as warm fluid dripped down my leg. *What is that?*

And then I knew what it was. *No one tells you anything!*

I found myself angry at every movie I'd ever seen. At every television show where a couple had sex. Where was the truth? Certainly not in them.

I cleaned up and put my clothes back on, then sat down on a chair, watching Kyle sleep. I didn't know what else to do.

I couldn't even think.

Chapter Three

I checked my watch. One hour and twelve minutes had passed when Kyle stretched, groaned, and woke up.

"Hi, babe!" he said when he saw me, a grin lighting up his face. "Are you glad you tried your first ice cream cone?"

I fake-smiled and lied. "Yeah. It was wonderful."

"C'mere." He beckoned with his finger.

I walked stiffly and sat on the edge of the bed. Kyle reached up and put his hands on my cheeks, pulling me down to give me a tender kiss. Instead of melting, I got mad. *How could someone kiss so sweetly and be so insensitive?*

Kyle interrupted my thoughts. "Why did you put your clothes on? You were beautiful without them."

Something tightened inside of me. "Oh? So I don't look beautiful with them on?"

"No, you know what I mean." He propped himself on his elbow. "Is something wrong?"

"I'm sorry, Kyle. It's . . ." I looked at the clock so I could lie again. "Oh, it's later than I thought. I need to get home to help Mom." I pecked him on the cheek and fled out the door.

I avoided all the main streets on the way home, I was so afraid I might meet someone I knew. I didn't want anyone to see me. All I wanted was to get home and into the shower. What would I say to my family? What would I do?

I sneaked up to my room and shed my clothes, tucking them in the back of the closet behind the long skirts I didn't wear anymore. I didn't want Mom to wash my clothes. I would have to offer to do all the laundry so she wouldn't see my underwear. I hate doing laundry. But I guessed anything was better than her finding out.

I hid until dinnertime, certain everyone would know just by looking at me. But they didn't. I bet for them it was a normal Saturday night.

All evening I wished I had agreed to sit for Jan. At her house I wouldn't have to paint on smiles and force acceptable conversation. Bedtime brought relief, at least from the presence of family. But sleep wouldn't come and deliver me from my rushing thoughts.

Each time I closed my eyes I could feel Kyle's body against mine. I could feel his motion. The motion that rubbed me raw inside and out.

What's wrong with me? I kept asking myself. *Why didn't I enjoy it?* I must have missed something to feel so confused and unsatisfied.

The rest of the week I tried to avoid Kyle. It didn't work. And I couldn't think of any excuse not to let him make love to me whenever he wanted. Each time I expected to experience the thrill of sex—you know, the thrill everyone always talks about.

The physical part hurt less. And I liked some things. But each time still disappointed me.

There was something missing that I couldn't put my finger on. Something I desperately wanted in my heart. That ache seemed to grow bigger while the physical hurt became smaller.

I did enjoy the affection. Kyle kissed, touched, and held me like I was something wonderful. His tender words softened my heart. "Julie, I love you," he would say over and over.

But soon he would become anxious, like he couldn't wait another second for his pleasure, and my pleasure lapsed into past tense.

"Sex changes your relationship," I had heard my friends' happy voices say more than once. Well, ours changed, all right. I got more sullen as Kyle demanded more and grew less fun.

He swept every spare moment of my life into his pocket as though it was all his. Before our "ice cream," I'd given those moments willingly, glad he wanted them. Now he grabbed them, almost without my permission.

One week. Two weeks. Another day, another request.

Kyle's eager voice greeted me as I answered the

phone. "Hi, hot stuff, how about meeting me for another ice cream?"

I wanted to turn him down but couldn't. Instead, I replied in mock excitement, "Of course, Kyle, that would be great." Hanging up the phone, I thought what a great little actress I'd become these past three weeks.

I found Mom and told her it was ice cream time again.

"Another ice cream?" she teased. "And so early in the morning! Kyle will go broke supporting your habit."

"Yeah, right," I said. If she only knew whose habit was really being supported.

"Jule, what's come over you lately?" Mom asked with concern. "Where's the cheerful girl I know? You're awfully irritable."

"Yeah, right," I repeated as I slammed the back door.

My feet hit the pavement hard as I walked to meet Kyle. I wanted to talk with someone about my situation. I couldn't talk with Stephanie. We didn't see each other much anymore. Sometimes it seemed I could barely remember what she looked like.

"Julie!"

The voice startled me. I spun around. "Jan. I haven't seen you in so long," I said, feeling nervous.

"I know," she said, smiling. "You've been so

preoccupied with Kyle you haven't had a chance to come even for a little visit. Right?"

I nodded, twirling a small clump of hair around my finger. "I'm sorry, Jan."

"That's okay, Julie. Stevie misses you."

As she spoke, I looked at the ground, bending and straightening my knee.

"Maybe you can stay away from Kyle long enough to baby-sit for us some day next week?"

My mind was so preoccupied, it took a moment to realize she had asked a question. "Of course," I answered, trying to sound eager.

"Julie, is something wrong?" Jan pierced me with concerned eyes.

"Not really." I knew I had to divert the conversation. Talking with Jan was my answer, but I didn't want her to know about Kyle and me. "I just heard Carol had her baby. A girl."

"Great!"

"She's living in The City with her aunt now. There are better job opportunities there." I paused, trying to think of the right way to put my next sentence. "But something about her situation bothers me. Can we talk?"

"Sure. Now?"

"No, I'm meeting Kyle now."

"How about tomorrow at one? We can go to Kramer's for an ice cream . . . my treat."

"Sure," I said, forcing a smile.

Funny how the thought of ice cream didn't please me as much as it used to. I didn't even like to think about it anymore.

But I couldn't exactly tell Jan that. Glancing at the bank's digital clock, I read 10:07, then 100 degrees. It was pretty well guaranteed another scorcher would come tomorrow, which meant there was no excuse to avoid ice cream.

———

"Hi, Stevie!" I said the next day as Jan arrived, pushing his stroller.

"Hi, Dulie!" Stevie shrieked in his little baby voice. "Ice cweam, ice cweam."

"In a minute," Jan replied, sounding impatient. She turned to me. "Kids are wonderful, but sometimes . . ." She sighed and shook her head. "It's been a hard day."

We bought our ice cream and went across the street to the park. I chose the bench furthest from the others.

"So what about Carol is bothering you?" Jan asked after the typical small talk.

I wiped my sweaty palms one at a time on the back of my cutoffs. "Her situation has made me think about . . . sex." I took a deep breath, trying to push the next words out. They felt heavy on my chest. "Do you . . . enjoy sex?" My voice cracked.

Not acting too surprised, Jan answered, "Sure, Julie, I love it. Why?"

I tried to act casual, licking my cone before I answered. I shrugged my shoulders. "I guess I just wondered what all the fuss is about. Why do people always seem to have sex on their minds? TV, movies, magazines—everybody is always talking about sex. I'm just wondering if it's really worth all the attention it gets."

Jan laughed. "Yes and no." She paused to give a bite of ice cream to Stevie. "It depends on your relationship. If the relationship is right, sex is very special and satisfying. If it's not, it's scary—filled with guilt and dissatisfaction."

"What do you mean, a 'right' relationship?" I leaned over and gave Stevie a bite from my cone.

"I mean a marriage based on love and trust and commitment. I know Rick loves me and won't leave me tomorrow. I don't have to engage in sex to keep him. He cares about what pleases me in our sexual relationship and carries it through."

"You can have all that trust, love, and commitment without marriage," I said with faked assurance. I knew I didn't have any of that with Kyle. No real security. Deep inside I was afraid it would be sex or good-bye. But I couldn't say that. "So how could it be wrong for someone to have sex just because they're not married?"

Jan shared more of her cone with a squirming Stevie. "Because God says it's wrong, and for good reasons. He knows us quite well. After all, He made us, and He made sex. So He ought to know what He's talking about."

"Okay. Give me some of the reasons."

Jan tilted her head, thinking. "God doesn't give us rules at random. They're designed to protect us, and for some very basic, practical reasons. For one thing, sex has an incredible power."

I stared at her. I knew what she meant, but pretended I didn't.

"The power of sex changes us. It can destroy people, control them. But in a marriage relationship it has the power to heal and strengthen and build up."

I didn't like where this was going. "You sound like a preacher or something."

Jan laughed. "I guess that's the result of being a youth pastor's wife." Jan crossed her legs on the bench. "On the practical side of why not have sex, there's the very real possibility of getting AIDS."

"Not if you're careful."

Jan frowned. "Careful isn't good enough, Julie."

"But if each person has been with only one person . . ."

"You don't always know if you're the only person. People have been known to lie about their sexual histories. The only way you can be sure is to have sex only within marriage."

It felt as if a hand were grasping my throat. I looked away, giving more ice cream to Stevie.

Jan continued. "AIDS isn't the only fear. There are a lot of other viruses and infections you can get—sexually transmitted infections."

"You mean STIs?" I said, trying to sound knowledgeable.

She nodded. "They're getting worse. Rick invited a doctor friend of ours to talk to our youth group, and he told about all these infections in teenage girls who've begun to have sex. Some of these STIs can be serious enough to cause cancer. Or sterility. And that means no babies. Ever."

I raised my eyebrows in mock interest but didn't say anything.

"Did you know that God has a great deal invested in your enjoyment of sex?"

"Oh, come on!" I said, stifling a laugh. "God doesn't want anyone to enjoy sex, does He?"

It was Jan's turn to laugh. "Of course He does. It's the ultimate symbol of His relationship with us."

I stared at her. "It is?"

She nodded, a smug smile on her face. "Yeah. People who don't know the Bible probably don't know that. God wants sex to be the greatest so we know He is the greatest. That His love for us is full of pleasure and fulfillment and fun. But He also wants us to see that there's only *one* God, and only *one* relationship that can have that kind of pleasure. That's why He set up marriage with only one person."

I'd never heard anything like this. I mean, I knew about God a little bit. I figured He was around somewhere. But I had this picture of Him trying to suck all the fun out of our lives.

"See, God didn't want the Israelites, who were His people, following after anything or anyone but Him," Jan added. "So He set up a covenant with them and called it a marriage between Israel and Him."

I could feel my eyes glazing over. Who cared about the Israelites? They sounded dusty and boring. Jan must have noticed. She switched tracks.

"Anyway, God created marriage as the perfect place to enjoy sex. In marriage, commitment is the shelter over your head. It protects your emotions and proves love."

I'd heard enough of the God talk. It was my turn to switch tracks. "But I've heard it's awful to marry a virgin," I protested. "Who wants to marry someone with no experience, and all that? How can I be a good lover for my husband if I don't practice first?"

Jan winced. "I've heard that, too. But it's not true. Being a virgin is something special, for girls *and* for guys. Then you come into marriage with only each other to learn from. You learn what pleases your husband, and you aren't distracted by what pleased someone else. You start fresh. There aren't painful memories to fight."

I looked down at the napkin in my hand. "Then why do guys push so hard to have sex?"

"Oh . . . because God made most males with an incredible sex drive. Once those hormones kick in, it isn't easy for guys to turn back. And if nobody's taught them responsibility and respect, they think whatever seems good for them must be good for everyone."

"Sounds like a music video I saw a couple of weeks ago."

"Well, sure. Don't a lot of movies and TV shows give you the idea that sex is something you shouldn't miss just because you're not married?"

I nodded. *Maybe Kyle's been watching too much MTV.*

Jan sighed. "Some guys are so wrapped up in their hormones they forget that the girl is a human being giving up a part of herself. Or they think of sex as a game they can 'score' in. Then it's purely selfish." She shook her head. "Sex is so much more than that."

"But not all guys are that way," I protested.

"No, they aren't. Some really do love and care. But without that lifelong commitment, even when a guy loves a girl, sex is still not all it's supposed to be. It's still lacking."

I knew too well what she was talking about. But I wasn't about to let on. "I . . . don't think I understand all this."

"I didn't either until I got married," Jan assured me. "I came to understand that sex is giving. Giving enjoyment to the one you love. Making him or her feel good. There's nothing wrong with that. God made our bodies in such a way that sex would make us feel good. When Rick and I got married, I was so glad for God's wisdom, even though it hadn't really made sense to me before."

"So you were a virgin when you got married?"

"Yes. Both Rick and I were."

I stared at her.

Jan grinned. "It wasn't easy, believe me! We survived only with God's help and a lot of prayer. And strict avoidance of backseats, bedrooms, empty houses, and thick shrubbery." She chuckled, then shook her head, looking into the distance. "It was so hard!"

She turned and looked me in the eyes. "But it was worth waiting. I have a lot of friends who didn't, and were sorry. Wait for sex, Julie—you won't regret it."

Regret? I could become a spokesgirl for regret.

"Thanks a lot, Jan," I said, thinking her advice had come too late.

"I'm always here for you, Julie. See you next Friday then?"

"Sure." I patted Stevie on the cheek, then kissed him. "Bye!"

As I walked home, a car rolled by, windows open—probably in a vain attempt to dispel the heat within.

"You are my fantasy," the radio blared, "my life, my love. I'll never leave you . . ."

I couldn't stop the tears.

Jan was right. There was only one way to stop hurting myself.

I knew I had to tell Kyle good-bye.

Chapter Four

"Kyle, I can't go on like this." I buried my face in his smooth chest.

He stroked my hair and my bare back. "Like what, hot stuff?"

"I—I want to break off our relationship."

"But why?" He sounded like a hurt puppy.

"I can't pretend anymore." I started to cry, and soon drenched his chest with my tears. "I can't pretend I get the same thing out of sex that you do, because I don't."

Instead of giving me the gentle understanding I expected, he grabbed my arms and pushed me away to where he could look into my face. "What do you mean you don't enjoy sex?" his voice pounded me. "What a stupid reason to destroy a good relationship!"

I just looked at him through blurry eyes, trying hard not to break into sobs.

He continued, "Sex with me is great! How can you *not* like it?"

At that moment I understood. "Your reputation is at stake, isn't it?" I almost shouted as I dried my cheeks. "If we break up, you're worried I'll tell someone you're bad in bed." I got out of bed and stomped over to the chair. I turned my back on him and pulled on my clothes.

As I turned to leave, I saw Kyle's lips were tight and his eyes narrow. He kept silent as he watched me go.

I don't remember walking home. I ignored my sister when I got there, going straight to the phone. I punched speed dial for Stephanie, but got my mom's newest friend instead. My hands shook as I took out the phone book and flipped the pages to LEWIS, P. I felt awful that I had forgotten her number.

"Stephanie," I asked, trying to sound cheerful, "want to go see a movie tonight?"

She paused for a long time. "What happened, Kyle go to The City?" she asked.

"No. I just thought . . . well . . . we haven't seen each other in a long time."

Her voice softened. "I'm sorry, Julie. I've felt so left out of your world."

"I know, Steph. I've left a lot of people out."

She rescued me. "I'll see you at seven, then?"

"Okay."

I was glad the movie was supposed to be sad. It gave me an excuse to cry through the whole thing. Afterward I struggled through an ice cream at Kramer's. I tried hard not to cry, yet another tear would slip out. I waited until Stephanie bent over her hot fudge before I wiped my face.

Then she caught me. "Come on, Julie, the movie wasn't *that* sad," she teased. She tilted her head to one side as the smile left her face. "What's bugging you?"

I looked at her and attempted to speak. "Oh, Steph . . ." Tears rushed down my face. I could only shake my head, grab my purse, and race out the door.

Looking over my shoulder I could see a confused Stephanie tripping over people and chairs in her attempt to follow me.

"Julie, Julie!" her voice pleaded in the darkness.

I continued to run until I turned a corner, certain she couldn't see me anymore. Slowing to a walk, I let my sorrow and anger flow unheeded. I wished I could talk to her. But we'd always ridiculed girls who'd made the same decisions I had. We'd mocked their weakness. Their stupidity. We called them sluts. Was that what I'd become? I couldn't face it. Not with Steph.

When I reached home the tears had dried, but my anger at Kyle and at myself still bubbled and boiled inside.

A small note, written on a torn-off corner of a magazine, had been tacked to our message board over the phone. "Call Kyle." I figured my sister, Tammy, must have taken the message. At 12, she couldn't be burdened with details.

As I wondered whether I should return the call and spit out my anger, the phone rang. "Hello?"

"Julie, I'm sorry."

Icicles laced my voice. "Me too, Kyle."

"No, Jule. I'm sorry I made you so angry. You know I love you."

The icicles melted just a little. "Do you? If you did, would you say those things?"

"I'm a jerk. I'm a guy. I would grovel if I could, but I'd scrape my knees and everyone would ask questions."

I tried not to smile. It didn't work.

"So? Forgive me?"

I tried to decide if I should cling to my anger or let it go.

"Pretty please? I'll dig a hole and crawl in it for as long as you want."

"Okay." Then the icicles were gone, and I blurted, "I love you, too."

"Then don't say good-bye."

He's right. I can't let him go.

Kyle the cunning. Kyle the fox. Kyle the master-piece. He held my heart firmly, yet gently, in his hand.

"I won't," I whispered.

"And, Julie, I understand. We can lay off the sex for a week."

"Thanks," I replied. But I knew he didn't

understand. He didn't have a clue. He probably thought my emotions were jumbled because of my period. I frowned at the thought. *What period?* I never kept track because I was so irregular anyway. But I didn't tell Kyle that it wasn't because of a period. I was too thankful for a week off from sex. I wished it could be longer, but didn't know how to ask.

I enjoyed every minute of that week. We chased kids off the swings, slides, and merry-go-round at the park so we could play. We called friends we hadn't seen in our previous weeks of being hermits. We planned bike rides and swimming get-togethers.

Stephanie was usually there, flirting with this guy or that one, always tossing her golden hair. Every so often she threw me a concerned look, which I ignored. I still pretended the tears were over the movie.

And then the week was done.

Our first time back in bed showed me nothing had changed. I tried to hide my discouragement. I made excuses to get out of there and home to where I could rummage through all my feelings.

One night, when I closed the door to my room, I turned on the sound system. I slid the CD Kyle had given me into the player. Clamping on the earphones, I lay on the floor with my feet up on my bed.

"I'll never leave you . . ." drifted from ear to ear. The motion reminded me of something.

Seesaws! I hadn't been on a seesaw in years. I couldn't believe I'd ever liked them. They gave you a funny feeling in the pit of your stomach—almost like you wanted to throw up, but not quite.

My eyes widened. The same feeling happened every time I saw Kyle! Up, down. Up, down. Churning inside. Wanting to love him, not loving him. Wanting sex, not wanting sex.

But like any seesaw, it was hard to stop once it got started. And I didn't have strength enough to stop this one.

My seesaw was up, and my life was filled with joy when we had our clothes on. When the clothes came off, the seesaw hit the ground with a jarring bump, jumbling my insides all over again.

"I AM NOT HAPPY!" I would scream to no one and everyone. But no one heard my silent voice.

———

And so the seesaw days of August passed, each differing only slightly from the one before. The first few days of September pulled in the Labor Day weekend on a towrope.

Being the official finale of summer, Labor Day stirred up our town more than any other weekend of the year. Kyle and I made sure we were a part of every activity available. Then it too was over.

By Monday night most of the tourists had gone home, freeing the popular eating spots from the crowds. Kyle and I trooped into the deli for a sandwich.

"Here we are again," I said, throwing out my arms.

Kyle's spark had disappeared. "Yeah."

"C'mon, spoilsport. Let's be romantic and relive our first date."

It was as if Kyle hadn't heard me. "I'm leaving tomorrow, hot stuff."

I stopped short. "Oh, for how long?"

"Julie, where's your head? I'm going home. You know, back to The City . . . senior year . . . all that stuff."

I couldn't believe it. Already? He was leaving. And not coming back.

"Oh." I waited for the sadness to hit, but all I felt was relief. *Why? I should be sobbing with grief.*

He touched my hand. "I don't know when I'll see you again, little one."

"Not tomorrow?"

"No. We have to leave early."

"Won't you be able to come visit on weekends?"

Kyle twisted his napkin into uselessness. "Well, Julie . . . I'm not sure my parents will . . . uh . . . let me come alone."

"Come on, Kyle. They leave you here for weeks

at a time alone. Why can't they let you drive? You're a big boy now." I sighed, unable to control my sarcasm. "It's only three hours."

Kyle touched my lips with the tips of his fingers to quiet me. "You know the boss. There's no arguing with him."

That was true. But I couldn't believe his dad wouldn't let him come see me. His dad called me "little darlin'" and always lectured Kyle on "The Care and Feeding of Julie."

Here was the seesaw again. One second I searched for ways for Kyle to visit; the next, relief flooded me that I'd be free. Free from the pressure and pleasure and pain and confusion.

We walked to my house, hand in hand, taking every long-cut possible. I looked at my watch. "Kyle, it's past my curfew. You can't come in."

"I know."

I turned to face him, taking his free hand in mine. "Kyle, I—"

I never finished my sentence. Kyle pulled my hands around his back, our fingers still laced together. He kissed the top of my head. Then as I looked up, we kissed once more.

He touched the tip of my nose with his index finger. "I love you, Julie. Bye." He walked a few steps, turned, and grinned. "Don't forget our song."

Just like that, he turned and left.

Nothing fit together. Not my emotions, not his

response. It didn't seem real that he'd be leaving the next day. He'd become a part of me. A day wouldn't seem right without him.

I knew love didn't end as easily as Kyle's good-bye. I turned to enter the house, confident he'd be back in a couple of weeks.

He wouldn't last without me.

Chapter Five

I'd blown it. All the time I'd known Jan, I'd listened with patience to her talk about Jesus. At least she didn't grab your collar, glare in your eye, and threaten you with hell if you didn't plead for mercy. You could tell Jesus was a big part of her life. She talked about Him in the same natural way that I talked about Kyle.

Anyway, I felt really bad that I'd laughed at her. I couldn't recall ever being so rude before.

It had happened the previous night, when I was keeping Jan company while Rick was out of town. We were talking about family stuff when I began to share some of my feelings that were bothering me.

"You know, Jan, sometimes I think nobody loves me."

She focused on the fabric moving through her sewing machine. "Why's that, Julie?"

"Oh, I don't know. Mom is so busy with work and all. She doesn't have much time to think of herself, much less me."

Jan nodded. "What about your dad?"

I shook my head, then began to twist my hair around my finger into a curl. "Dad is so quiet. Mom says his construction work wears him out.

She says that he pours himself into his work so much that he doesn't have anything left for us when he gets home. Sometimes it seems the only time I hear his voice is when he's yelling at a referee or somebody on TV."

Jan looked up from her sewing, her eyes tender. "Julie, I think you know deep inside that they love you."

"Yeah, I guess so." I tapped my foot on the floor, avoiding her eyes. "I wish they would show it more often."

I looked up. Jan bent her head over her sewing again.

"Why can't we always be loved? I want Kyle to love me always, but he hasn't called."

Jan looked up. "It's only been one day."

I threw her a look. She laughed. "Sorry. I'd forgotten how long one day can be."

"Thank you," I said.

"What about IM?"

"Instant messaging?" I shook my head. "Dad caught my brother, Matt, looking at porn on the Internet, and freaked out. My parents put some hefty filters on the computer. We're not even allowed to e-mail now, much less IM." I sighed. It wasn't fair, having to pay the price for Matt's stupidity.

Jan's kind, green eyes searched mine. "Julie, I have a friend who loves you all the time. He never forgets to be there when you need to talk."

"Who?"

"Jesus."

I burst into laughter. How silly. Someone I didn't even know or believe in loved me? No way.

Now I stood in our upstairs bathroom, thinking about laughing at her last night. I supposed I should apologize. I paused, tapping my hairbrush on the palm of my hand as I pondered my own suggestion.

Then, brushing again with a vengeance, I decided to apologize later. After all, today was the first day of school. I had a lot to think about.

By the time I left the house, I'd put the whole thing on a shelf in the back closet of my mind.

Stephanie waited for me at the corner. "Why so glum?" I asked, dressing my words with saccharine cheer.

She heaved a loud sigh as we trudged our way in the leftover summer heat. "The first day of school must be the worst day of the year."

"Almost," I answered, fanning myself with my new spiral notebook. "There's only one group of days that could rate lower."

"When's that?"

I held my breath a moment for effect, then let the word escape: "Finals."

"You got it." She began to laugh. "How could I forget?"

With Kyle gone, our conversation again flowed with the ease of the "old days."

We found seats in homeroom together and waited for the teacher to hand out our class schedules for the year.

Jenny Wilkinson sat down near us. "Hi, Stephanie. Hi, Julie. How's Kyle?"

"Fine, I guess. He's only been gone two days." Turning to Stephanie, I said, "That's at least the tenth person who has asked."

"Don't I know it," she hissed. "No one cares how I feel, only about Kyle."

"Don't get so riled," I zipped back. "You must notice they don't ask about me, either."

I thought that would lighten her mood, but Stephanie looked angrier than ever. I couldn't understand why she always looked like that when someone mentioned Kyle's name.

"Okay, Steph, we'll change the subject," I said. "Besides, here comes Mr. Silva."

The teacher passed out schedules by intoning last names. "Landon, Lathrop, Leffingwell, Lewis . . ."

Stephanie and I were studying her schedule when Rachael Muñoz, sitting behind me, tapped my shoulder. "You're next," she whispered.

"Madden, Marshall . . ."

I jumped and tripped over my own feet. The class choked back laughter as I grabbed my schedule and managed a more graceful return.

"What classes do you have?" Stephanie asked.

I whispered back, "English lit., government with Mr. Silva, math, PE, and Spanish."

"Great, we have first and third periods together."

"Yeah, much better than last year." I jumped as the end-of-class bell sounded. "I'd better get used to those bells again."

"What are you doing after school?" Stephanie asked on the way to our next class. "Would you like to come over for a while?"

"Thanks, Steph, but I've been so tired the last couple weeks. I think I'll go home and take a little nap."

"A nap? Are you serious?"

I nodded, embarrassed. Then I changed the subject. "I'm glad school begins on Wednesday. It sure makes the week go faster."

"A *nap?*" Stephanie repeated, tossing her golden hair. I hadn't fooled her at all.

After school I went straight home. I gave the message to Tammy that I would be in my room under the influence of my earphones should Kyle call. Then I disappeared into seclusion, listening to our song as I fell asleep.

"Julie, Julie. Wake up."

The CD had ended, and I looked up to see my mom tapping her finger on her watch. "Is it Kyle?"

I asked, yanking the earphones off and reaching across my bed toward the phone.

"No, it's dinnertime. Now come on, sleepy-head."

Mom's kindness didn't continue the rest of the week as she had to wake me up for dinner every night and hassle me for not doing my daily chores. "Are you staying up late, Julie? I don't want to give you a bedtime like a small child, but if this keeps up—"

I felt bad that I fell asleep so much. But I was so tired that I couldn't help it. I figured the new school routine threw my system off.

Each night after dinner as I did my homework, I kept the cordless next to me so I could answer it the moment it started to ring. I always spoke in my sexiest voice, hoping to hear Kyle's in return—but each time left me filled with disappointment.

By Sunday night I was wild with tension and impatience. Desperation to call Kyle consumed me. But my old-fashioned, never-call-a-boy daddy would see Kyle's long-distance number on the bill.

I'd have to get a phone card. But not working a job this summer—and spending all my baby-sitting money on school clothes—meant I was nearly broke. I stared at the $10 bill in the top drawer of my dresser. I reminded myself that I was saving it for an absolute emergency. I closed the drawer against temptation. Maybe someday I'd learn to think ahead.

I tried not to think about the ache I felt for Kyle. Crawling into bed, I sighed. At least in school it was easier to distract myself.

————

Monday morning I dragged myself out of bed only 20 minutes before I had to meet Stephanie for school. It didn't help that I'd disrupted my sleep to get up and use the bathroom twice during the night.

I grabbed a piece of toast for breakfast, not having time or appetite for much else. I ran out the door and up to the corner.

"I was ready to give up on you," Stephanie called before I reached her.

"I'm sorry. I overslept," I answered, still a little groggy.

"I've noticed you look a little uneasy during math. Are you sleepy then, too, or having trouble with the work?"

Swallowing the last bite of toast, I wiped my mouth and answered, "No. I've been feeling a little sick to my stomach. I guess since it's right before lunch, my empty stomach makes me nauseated."

I didn't tell her that the math-class sensation bothered my mind more than my body. It mystified me. I'd never liked math before, but this sensation was too weird. Every day in class I got the incredible urge to throw up. I would chew gum, pant gently through my mouth—anything until the feeling passed. The weirdest thing is that it didn't happen in any other class. Only math.

Outside of class, I got the same feeling if anyone around me ate tuna. Just the smell of the stuff made me feel so sick I had to leave the area. I'd always adored tuna. But now . . .

I shook my head, not having the energy to think about it.

When Stephanie and I arrived at school, people asked about Kyle again. Too embarrassed to say I hadn't talked to him since he'd left, I'd answer, "He's fine."

Stephanie looked at me after about the fourth questioner had left. "How can you say, 'He's fine'?" she mimicked. "You haven't even heard from the creep."

The tone of her voice shook me. What made her so mad at Kyle?

"Is this going to be the pattern for the first day of every week?" she muttered.

We said nothing more and didn't even pass notes in class. I waved good-bye and threw in a grin before heading off to government. I knew things would be okay when a weak smile touched her lips and crept into her eyes.

As I sat in class I began to feel uneasy again. My bladder felt like it was about to explode. The feeling grew despite my efforts to ignore it and listen to Mr. Silva.

"Does anyone here like school?" a vibrant Mr. Silva questioned.

No answer.

"Come on. School is a fun way to gain the education needed to meet the growing demands of the world. The future is yours, and you must have the education to properly deal with that future to give an excellent world to your children."

I squirmed in my seat. My hand fluttered in the air like a butterfly.

"Yes, Miss Marshall. You like to meet the challenge of education head-on?"

I gulped. "Well, uh, Mr. Silva, I guess so . . . but at the moment, I'd rather meet the bathroom."

His face flushed as the class tittered. "Of course, Miss Marshall. You may be excused."

"Now class, how can we . . ." Mr. Silva's voice faded as I almost ran down the hall.

I couldn't understand why I couldn't seem to make it through a simple couple of classes without going to the bathroom. I'd developed a new habit of going there before each class period. When I skipped that detour, I'd find myself fighting the desperate need to excuse myself during class.

Even my friends noticed my problem.

"Hey, Julie, are you thinking of buying the john?"

"You spend more time in the hole than you do in class."

"Come on, Marshall, you can't get an A in bathroom attendance."

Even Stephanie joked until I told her I'd been having cramps for a couple of weeks and expected my period anytime. Of course, cramps were a normal part of my life as a "woman." And while going to the bathroom every hour wasn't part of that routine, I figured since the cramps were getting stronger and more painful and lasting longer, maybe they were increasing my need for trips to the tile cave.

Whatever the reason, it was getting old. Fast.

That morning Stephanie and I met for break. Long ago we'd set up a routine of devouring cinnamon rolls every day at that time, so we planted ourselves at a table and pulled pieces of the warm, sweet bread to pop into our mouths.

Stephanie shook her hair back from her face. "Julie, why is your mom putting a weeknight curfew on you?"

"She says if I'm too tired to do chores or homework before dinner, then I can stay home and do them after dinner."

"It doesn't seem quite fair."

I shrugged my shoulders. "It's okay. I'm so tired that I really don't care. I figure when I adjust to school, then I'll fight for my rights."

"You can't go *anywhere?*" she asked, shifting on the bench.

"Nope. Not even to baby-sit for Jan. I have to be in bed by nine-thirty."

"At least your mom doesn't know about the naps you take in class," Stephanie teased.

"I know."

We finished our cinnamon rolls and headed toward a group of friends.

"How's your PE class?" Stephanie asked. "You're playing volleyball, aren't you?"

"Yes, and I love it. That's my trophy sport, remember?" Before we reached our friends, I grabbed her arm and lowered my voice. "I hate the days just before my period," I murmured.

"Me too. What's your worst?"

"All the discomfort." Stephanie nodded as I elaborated. "Like my breasts. The nipples are real tender. They hurt a lot when I run or jump during the game. I feel like I'm going through puberty again."

"Maybe your chest has finally decided to follow your mother's genes instead of your father's," she quipped.

Letting her arm loose, I joined the group. "Thanks a heap," I shot over my shoulder to her.

That afternoon I felt that I had no sooner curled up on my bed when Tammy tugged on one of the earphone wires. "Kyle wants to talk to you," she announced, handing me the phone and marching off.

Shaking my head, trying to awaken my sleepy brain, I rolled over and stuck the phone next to my ear. "Hi, sweetie," I muttered.

"Well, hello, hot stuff. You sound like you've been dragged through the woods."

"Yeah. I mean, no. I've been asleep."

"Asleep! In the middle of the day?"

"Yeah," I said, yawning. "It's been real strange. I'm so sleepy all the time. I take a nap every day after school."

"School's too rough on you, huh?"

"I don't think so. That's why I don't understand this." I stretched. Waking up a little more, I asked, "Why haven't you called?" It was more of a plea than an accusation.

"Oh, you know how busy the first week of school is."

"I never thought of the first week as busy." I allowed my hurt feelings to come across.

"My, aren't we snippy today?" Kyle said, then laughed softly. The sound melted me.

"Okay, no excuses," he said. "I'm sorry. Now, how's school?"

"All right, I suppose. Except government. I could live without that." Then I blurted, "When do I get to see you again?"

Kyle paused for a long time, and I knew I had said the wrong thing. In a strained voice he answered, "I don't know . . ."

I tried again. "Kyle, I miss you."

"Yeah. . . . I'll call you on Thursday. Bye."

"Kyle, wait—" But he had already hung up the phone.

I felt empty—emptier than before he called. I sat on the floor, hugging my knees and dropping my head to rest on them. Crying didn't help much, but I couldn't stop myself.

A minute later the phone rang again. I jumped to answer it, hoping Kyle had decided to call back. "Hello," I said.

"Well, hello there. What are you so excited about?" Jan asked.

My joy crashed on the floor, and I began to cry.

"Julie, are you there?"

As best I could, I answered, "Yeah, Jan, I'm here."

"What's wrong?"

"Kyle just called."

"That should make you happy."

"I know, but it didn't. I feel worse than before he called. All we said was hello and good-bye and that I wouldn't see him for a while."

"I'm sorry, Julie. Would it help for you to come over?"

"No, I'll be okay."

"I'm calling to ask if you want to baby-sit for Stevie on Saturday night."

"You mean you aren't mad?"

"About what?"

"Me laughing at what you said about Jesus."

"Of course not."

"I wanted to apologize . . ."

"There's no need to. Can you sit? Rick is tak-ing me to the Smokehouse Inn for dinner."

"Ooooh, how nice. I'd love to. What time?"

"Be here at five-thirty?"

"Sure."

"Are you sure you're okay?" Jan's voice sounded concerned.

"Oh, I don't know. My body has been so weird." Then my words began to tumble out, almost of their own accord. "I sleep a lot, have cramps like I'm going to start my period, only worse. I eat like a pig, I can't eat tuna, I go to the bathroom every hour and at least twice during the night. Math makes me sick, literally. I cry one minute, laugh the next, and have headaches in between."

For the first time, I'd thrown all my complaints together. Suddenly I wished I could stuff the words back into my mouth. How could I be so stupid? I stopped, not knowing how to continue. Jan paused for a long, long time. She was so quiet I thought maybe she'd left. "Jan?"

Her voice was soft. "Julie, it sounds like you're pregnant. Is that possible?"

"Of course not," I burst in, trying to hide the fear I felt. "I don't have any of the symptoms. You have to get fat and throw up every morning. But most important, you have to have sex to get pregnant."

Then I added, with a false confidence I hoped she wouldn't detect, "I'm sure I'll start my period tomorrow."

I didn't want Jan to have another chance to say anything, so I said, "I'll see you Saturday night. Make sure you have something for Stevie and me to scarf on while you're gone." I hung up.

Looking in the mirror, I pulled up my shirt and looked at my belly. Front and side views. Nothing looked different—*but my last period was a long time ago.* I had my last one right after I met Kyle. Around the beginning of July sometime.

Then reason spoke. *Julie, this is September. You should be having another period. It's been eight weeks.*

I gasped, dropped my shirt, and covered my mouth. Stifling a sob, I whispered, "Oh, God, please, no. Please."

Chapter Six

Sometimes I hate the night. Suspicions grow into enormous monsters—distorted and threatening. That night as I tried to fall asleep, I couldn't seem to get comfortable. I flip-flopped like a fish out of water. When I tired of that, I held still while my mind continued the motion. Fatigue finally won the battle until a short time later, when morning appeared.

The early sun always chased away the monsters. I decided my fears were only fantasies, imaginings. The idea of me being pregnant was ridiculous. Preposterous. I couldn't be. I'd certainly know if I were.

I felt good the next two days, excluding, of course, the minor complaints of my body.

Kyle kept his promise to call on Thursday. *What a sweetie*, I thought.

But I knew not to mention him coming to see me, though my heart ached—no, was dying—to ask him to come.

We talked about his school and our families. Chitchat about life's little routines. Then my emotions took charge.

"Kyle, I miss your touch."

"Yeah, hot stuff? I miss yours, too."

My heart warmed. I wanted to touch him, to caress him, but especially to kiss him.

"Are you still there?" he asked.

"Yes," I murmured. "I'm still here. But I wish I were there."

"Feeling's mutual." He paused for a second. "Listen to our song and think of me, okay?"

"Sure will."

"Bye, hot stuff."

"Bye."

After listening to "I'll Never Leave You" three times, I floated down the stairs to set the table for dinner. Mom's eyes opened wide with unasked questions. I hadn't exactly been Cheri Cheerful lately. But I didn't offer any explanations because I didn't want anything to break the bubble of joy surrounding me.

I slipped into the dining room, taking a stack of plates from the cupboard. I put each one in position, singing quietly, "You are my fantasy, my life, my love. I'll never leave you for another . . ."

Tammy walked into the room and heard my song. She rolled her eyes as she said, "I am so sick of that song. It is *so* played out."

I simply smiled and sang a little louder, "You are the one forever and today. You are the one for always . . ."

Tammy stuffed her fingers in her ears and made a hasty exit.

The song kept on in my heart even after dinner had begun. I felt happy, listening to the flow of conversation around the table. Nothing could get me down.

"Dinner sure is good, Mom," I said, loading another pile of green beans onto my plate.

The clinking sounds of forks against plates ceased. I looked up to discover the reason for the unusual silence. Everyone was staring at me.

"What are you all looking at?" I asked.

"We aren't used to seeing you eat that much, Julie," Mom said in awe.

"What much?"

"Three helpings, to be exact. Of everything."

"What's wrong with three helpings? Matt eats at least four at every meal."

"Yes, but your brother is a growing boy. He's supposed to eat a lot."

"If growing sons can eat a lot, why not growing daughters?" I asked, shoveling another bite into my mouth.

Dad leaned forward, his chest inches from his plate. "When barely-one-helping Julie begins to eat three helpings, we get curious, that's all."

I shrugged without missing a bite.

"You might think about cutting down on all that food," Mom said, "unless you're hinting for a whole new wardrobe two sizes larger."

Her words set my mind to work. My pants

were beginning to get a little tight. I often unzipped my jeans when I sat down. I had even worn dresses to school the last couple of days to be more comfortable.

During the summer, Mom had said if I wasn't careful, I would get fat from all the ice cream cones Kyle was giving me . . .

I put my fork down, not hungry anymore. Fear chased away my appetite, filling my stomach. Fear that Kyle's "ice cream" really had made me fat. And the other night Jan had suggested the same thing. As the thoughts shot around inside my head, I knew I had to find out. An idea burrowed its way into my mind.

"Mom, don't forget I have to baby-sit for Jan Saturday night."

"I hadn't forgotten. I'll need your help cleaning the house before you go."

"Okay. Do you mind if we do it in the afternoon? I'd like to go to the library in the morning to study."

"Go ahead. Plan to be home by noon."

I nodded, then excused myself.

Fear nestled deeper and deeper inside me. Sleep came in restless snatches. The week dragged until Friday appeared, holding an eternity of questions that I hoped would be answered soon.

Saturday brought no change of heart, only a change of scenery. Even the peace of the library couldn't dispel the fear growing inside me. I approached the computer catalog and typed in the word *pregnancy*. It figured. There had to be hundreds of books on the subject.

The call number 612 appeared most often for the books on pregnancy. The other books dealt with subjects related to pregnancy: birth, nutrition, parenthood, and sexuality.

I walked up and down the canyons of books, peering around the corners, hoping no one would be anywhere near the section dealing with pregnancy.

"May I help you?" A soft voice surprised me from behind.

I thought for sure the librarian could hear my heart thumping as I stuttered, "Uh, no. No, thanks. Here's what I'm looking for." I pointed to a section of books which turned out to be medieval history.

She nodded and walked away.

I waited until she had returned to her desk before continuing my search.

The first book I pulled from the shelf was a large, thick one entitled *Pregnancy*. I read the chapter titles, flipped through it, and looked in the index. The only symptoms it spoke of were "increased blood supply" and "softening of the uterus." Disgusting. All technical stuff. I didn't care about increasing blood supplies or what my uterus was up to. I only wanted to find out if I was pregnant.

The second book was just as thick, but at least

one chapter sounded promising: "Maybe You Are Pregnant." It, too, had more words than I cared to read, most of them big, long, thick ones, creeping across the pages like fuzzy caterpillars.

I decided to give up. This whole fiasco took at least an hour and a half. People continually walked down the aisle, and I would have to hide the book under my notebook. I'd never realized what a busy place our small library is.

There had to be another way to find out.

I worked like a whirlwind for Mom when I got home. I knew if I worked fast and hard, I wouldn't think about all the ifs plaguing me.

The ifs chased me all the way to Jan's house. Her face smiled a greeting, but her green eyes showed concern. She said nothing about our conversation on Monday, yet she must have sensed the questions lurking in the corners of my mind.

"Julie, after Stevie goes to bed, if you'd like, you are welcome to look at the books we have. There are quite a variety of subjects there. You might find something interesting."

Our eyes locked in silent understanding.

"Thanks," I said with more enthusiasm than necessary.

I felt guilty about putting Stevie to bed early, but my eagerness to see Jan's books enveloped me. I ran my fingers along the bindings, looking for anything promising. Two titles caught my eye. I reached out, hesitant, my finger lying on the top of the book. I took a deep breath and slid the first one out. My heart raced as I did the same with the second.

Neither helped much. Discouragement filled my heart as I replaced them on the shelves. Both spoke of dealing with morning sickness, constipation, and frequency of urination.

So what about all the other symptoms that attacked me daily? Were they connected to pregnancy?

"Oh, help," I said aloud.

I sat cross-legged on the floor, staring dubiously at the shelves. Another book caught my eye: *Family Medical Encyclopedia.* Why not? I grabbed it and turned to the table of contents. Pregnancy, chapter eight.

I read and reread the section on body changes. They listed the same symptoms as the other books, but added breast changes and tiredness.

Going back to the beginning of the chapter, I read the entire thing. I had to use Jan's dictionary to look up many of the words. As I read, the things I learned in health class last year took shape. I began to understand what the teacher had tried to explain to a class of blushing, giggling nitwits.

The thing that surprised me most was that conception—when pregnancy begins (I had to look that one up)—happens two weeks following a period. Usually. I'd always thought midmonth was the safe time when you couldn't get pregnant.

The book also discussed pregnancy tests sold in drugstores. It said anyone could buy them, and you didn't need a prescription. *A home test.* I hit my head with my hand. Of course! I'd seen all those goofy commercials with couples waiting to see if the line was blue or pink! Why hadn't I thought of that before? A home test would be perfect. No one would know about my possible pregnancy but me.

Maybe I could get one of those tests with that $10 bill from my dresser drawer. If anything was an emergency, this was it.

Jan took me home that night. We didn't say much, and when we got to my house, she looked at me, taking my hands in hers. Her smile echoed in her eyes. "No matter what happens to you, I want you to know I care." I looked away as she continued, "Jesus is also waiting to help you."

I nodded as if I knew what she was talking about. "Bye," I muttered, slipping from the car.

■——■

Monday passed as slow and grouchy as Friday. Poor Stephanie. Her constant efforts to cheer me up failed. I nodded as though I was paying attention.

After school I walked by the drugstore twice. Then, taking a deep breath, I pushed open the door. A bell tinkled, signaling everyone inside to look at me. I painted on my best smile, and scanned the area for any acquaintances. No familiar faces caught my eye, but to be safe I headed first for the greeting cards. I took my time browsing, all the while checking out every person in the store. I chose a couple of cards as a cover.

I sauntered through the aisles, making my way to the feminine hygiene section. I hated to go there any day, but my purpose this time caused me to be extra embarrassed, extra cautious.

It took me a moment to find the pregnancy test kits. I didn't know what to look for and was surprised to see how small the boxes were and the strange names on them. What does EPT mean, anyway? Most cost ten dollars or more. A store brand cost about seven. I shoved the greeting cards under my arm as I reached for the first box and began to read it. I shifted my weight from side to side, so nervous I could hardly see the words.

Just then, someone came down the aisle. Panicking, I shoved the box back on the shelf and reached for a box of minipads, pretending to be engrossed in the detail written there.

The woman paid no attention to me and meandered through, picked something from the shelf, and left. As I replaced the box of minipads, I noticed a brochure telling in more detail about one of the pregnancy tests. I shoved it into my purse and headed for the cashier. As I opened my purse to produce change for the greeting cards, I realized the pamphlet was in full view. I feigned searching for change as I shoved the pamphlet deep into my purse.

Muttering an obscure thank you, I grabbed my package and burst outside into the hot sunshine. I walked to my favorite hideaway in a nearby alley, hid in a shadow, and leaned against the cool brick building. I pulled the pamphlet from my purse, reading each word carefully. It said the test would be accurate the first day your period didn't show up. Three drops of urine were to be put in a plastic test case they provided. Within two to three minutes, you have your answer.

Sure, it was simple, but how would I buy it without anyone seeing? I groaned. *Where would I hide it at home?* I remember a sitcom where someone discovered her friend's pregnancy by seeing the empty box in the trash. No, a home pregnancy test was out.

Shredding the pamphlet, I let the pieces scatter in the breeze. I leaned against the wall again, searching the sky as if I would find the answer there.

I remembered Jan's book also spoke of pregnancy testing done in clinics and that some of them were free. I went to the library again to use their phone book.

I flipped to the heading "Clinics" in the yellow

pages. There were about five listed. I chose a Family Planning Clinic located in the next town. I couldn't risk the chance of being seen at the one in our town.

I wrote down only the phone number, tucking it into the hiding place in my wallet. I walked a long time before finding a phone booth in an area that didn't have people milling about. I took the number out, and my shaking fingers put some coins in the slot.

I waited what seemed an eternity for someone to answer. "Family Planning Clinic," a cheerful voice rang out.

"Umm, I, uh, wondered about, um, a pregnancy test."

The woman's voice never faltered. "Certainly. We have an available opening tomorrow morning. Is eight-forty-five okay for you?"

"Yes, I guess so."

"Name?"

I paused.

"Any name."

"Sandra."

"See you tomorrow, Sandra."

"Yeah," I said as she hung up.

Fear tightened its grip on my heart as I reluctantly headed for home.

Chapter Seven

I'd read in one of the books on pregnancy that a pregnancy test is most accurate if you use your first urine of the morning. Gross. But I decided I wanted to be sure, so I figured my best bet was to take some with me.

I knew Mom saved everything from Cool Whip bowls to ribbons from packages. I went to her stash in the garage and found a small mustard jar. I washed it on the sly, then hid it in my underwear drawer.

I set the alarm for six A.M. and spent the rest of the night checking the clock every half hour or so. I didn't want to miss the chance to get to the bathroom and secretly urinate in the jar.

Nothing went wrong until I returned to my room. I hadn't thought about how to transport the jar, unseen, to the clinic.

The possibilities weren't too promising. I didn't care to share my lunch sack with a leaky jar. Nor did I enjoy the thought of any spilling into my purse. Eau de Urine is not my favorite scent to carry around with me.

I decided to put the jar into two Ziploc bags, then a brown bag for cover.

Thirty minutes before Mom needed to leave for work, I went to her. I crouched over, gripping a chair, twisting my face into one of obvious pain.

"Mom, I've got real bad cramps," I lied. "Can you have Mrs. Anderson take you to work? When I get to feeling better, I can drive to school."

She looked at me a moment and sighed. "I guess so."

She pulled a heating pad from her cupboard. "Use this until you feel better."

"Thanks," I groaned. I handed her a paper and pen. "Better write me an excuse for school."

She nodded, scribbling her message.

"Bye, Mom." I kissed her cheek and crept to my bedroom. I plugged in the heating pad and curled up on the bed. I wanted to be ready in case she decided to check on me before she left.

I could hear her muffled voice talking on the phone. As soon as I heard the strange car pull up, and the front door slam, I jumped out of bed and got dressed.

The minute I got the car started, I turned the radio on, adjusting the tuner to KBAY.

I eased the car into the street and around the corner. Three blocks later the ear-filling roar flooded my brain with music, allowing no chance for thoughts to sneak their way in.

Then, without warning, a familiar tune filled the car. "You are my fantasy . . ." My heart leapt in my chest as my stomach turned upside down. Catching my breath, I turned the radio off as though it had sent fire through the car.

Then I saw the sign ahead: FAMILY PLANNING CLINIC. I bit my quivering lip as I pulled into a parking space, then paused a moment, gazing at the ugly, old, block-shaped concrete building before me.

Determined, I stuffed the brown bag into my purse and walked up the cracked cement steps to a large wooden door.

I stepped into the sunlit room and glanced around. I stared at the ugly green-and-white speckled linoleum. Pockmarks evidenced years of chairs scraping across the floor. The chairs that now were set in a semicircle were different sizes and styles. A couple were already occupied by unhappy-looking girls.

Although old, the room was spotless. It smelled of old paint and the musk of freshly watered plants. The receptionist smiled as she took my fake first name. "It will be about 15 minutes. Go ahead and sit down." She nodded her head toward the group of chairs.

I thanked her and headed for the chair furthest from the other waiting girls. It commanded a view of all sides of the room. I eased onto the black leatherette, clutching my purse as though the jar within contained gold.

Short, dark hair framed the face of the girl opposite me. Her leg bounced up and down. One hand held a magazine as she chewed the nails of the other.

I fanned myself with a magazine I'd found in the chair next to me. I glanced at the girl seated to my left.

She stared at the ground, pulling her sweater tighter around her trembling figure. Just looking at her caused the warm room to feel hot. I fanned faster and noticed my leg, too, bounced an uneasy rhythm.

A woman dressed in Levis and a light-blue blouse came out of a doorway and called a name. The girl with jagged fingernails jumped up from her chair.

About 10 minutes had passed when the girl returned, and a smile had changed her expression from one of despair to one of relief. She held a flat, oval plastic case in her hand. Her step seemed lighter than when she had gone in.

Another name was called, and the cold girl with the blank stare jumped as if she had been poked in the ribs. She looked up, a question on her face, then dragged her feet as she followed the woman in Levis.

As soon as she left, a couple more women entered through the front door. They seemed much older than I. One of the women smiled at me, but I turned away as if I didn't see her.

The inner door opened again, revealing a young woman in her late twenties. She, too, wore jeans with a casual, Hawaiian-print shirt. She ran her fingers through her long blonde hair as she looked at a card in her hand. "Sandra," she said.

I sat a moment, forgetting that was my name. Then I gathered my things and tried to stride to the door with confidence. Who did I think I was kidding?

As we entered, we passed the girl with the blank stare. Only now her eyes were red, and her face was smudged with running makeup. She pulled her sweater around her little figure and entered a door marked Counseling.

The woman I followed glanced over her shoulder and introduced herself. "Hi, Sandra. My name is Ann. My office is right down here."

"My name is really Julie."

She smiled. "Nice to meet you, Julie."

"I brought some urine from first thing this morning—you know, so it would be more accurate," I told her, taking my sack from my purse.

"It doesn't really matter anymore," she said. "Any time of day is fine."

I felt myself blush.

"It's okay," she said as she led me into her office. "Since you have it, we'll go ahead and use it."

We entered Ann's small office and she motioned me to sit on a large, wooden chair on one side of an old, massive, walnut desk set in the center of the room. A white metal cabinet sat in one corner. She reached into her creaking file cabinet and pulled out a few papers.

"Okay, Julie, we need to ask some questions before we do the test. Everything is confidential, but we do need accurate information. Fair?"

I nodded.

"Date of birth?"

"January twenty-first."

"Age now?"

"Sixteen."

"Have you had any previous pregnancies?"

"No."

"When was your last menstrual period?"

I thought for a while, trying to remember. "Around July eleventh."

"Were you using any form of birth control?"

"No."

Her eyebrows rose with a questioning pause. "Julie," she asked gently, "why didn't you use birth control? At the very least, why didn't you protect yourself from AIDS?"

I wanted to feel uncomfortable telling this stranger about my sex life when I hadn't told Stephanie or even Jan. But her question slipped out like it was as common as talking about the weather.

I took a deep breath and let the words tumble in a pile. "Well, I never even thought of AIDS because only gays and people like that get it. Kids don't get AIDS unless they're born with it, and he was my first and only . . . well . . . you know . . . so I didn't think of it and I knew you couldn't get pregnant the first time, and since my periods are so irregular . . . I mean, sometimes I go for two or three months between . . . so I thought I couldn't get pregnant very easily. Besides, I didn't know what I could use or where to get it."

Ann folded her hands, resting them on the desk. "Julie, anyone who has sex is able to get AIDS. Or any of the other STIs. Do you know about HPV?"

I shook my head.

"Most people don't. It's the most common sexually transmitted organism in the entire U.S. It causes some terrible complications, and it's connected with genital cancer in both sexes. In fact, cancers associated with HPV can and do kill more women every year than AIDS."

I didn't know what to say. It all sounded so scary and terrible. I just couldn't believe any of that could have happened to me. *Yeah, right,* a little voice said inside, *just like you couldn't believe you'd get pregnant.* I swallowed hard.

"Then there's herpes," Ann said.

"I've heard of that."

"Do you know there is no cure for herpes? It ranges from being a mildly irritating recurring disease to being a major, painful problem."

I shook my head again. My heart beat faster as she listed more diseases: chlamydia, gonorrhea, syphilis. I knew about some, but not that they were becoming resistant to the treatments doctors had always used against them. And not that they could affect my life forever. My stomach moved, and I felt like I might get sick.

"Condoms are crucial to protection from these diseases, but even condoms cannot guarantee you will not catch any of them."

"It all sounds so horrible."

"It can be. And on top of all that, you *can* get pregnant the first time you have sex. All irregular periods do is make it difficult to know when you ovulate, meaning the time when it is possible to get pregnant. Irregular periods do not mean you can't get pregnant.

"Before you leave today we will help you decide which method of birth control would be best for you from now on. Whatever we choose, we'll include condoms as protection against AIDS and other STIs."

I looked down at my lap and said in a small voice, "I don't expect to have sex again."

"Most girls don't. But sometimes, when the situation comes up, it's tough to refuse. Birth control is very important. It's better to be protected than pregnant."

I still didn't want any birth control, but now

she had aroused my curiosity. "What kind of stuff is there?"

"First there are the drugstore varieties, available right off the shelf, even in some supermarkets or department stores." She ticked off on her fingers, "Foam, jellies, creams, condoms, sponges, and suppositories. All of these must be used immediately before intercourse."

I interrupted, "I'm sorry to be so dumb, but exactly what is intercourse?"

"That is the actual putting the penis into the vagina. You aren't dumb. Many people don't know the meaning of the word.

"Back to birth control. Second are the prescription methods." She began to tick off on her fingers again. "The transdermal patch, the Depo-Provera injection, and, of course, the pill.

"The patch is placed on your body and remains there for seven days, when it's replaced by another patch. After three patches, you go seven days without a patch so you can have a period.

"Some physicians don't like to use Depo-Provera on teens. But it's a shot given once every three months.

"The pill is taken every day for twenty-one days with a pause for seven days to allow the period to come. Some varieties of pills have a sugar pill to take during the pause. This way you don't forget to begin the birth control pills again.

"The diaphragm and cervical cap are used along with creams or jellies. It is a small rubber dome which fits over your cervix. It must be fitted to your body by a doctor. You place it into your vagina up to six hours before intercourse, and should not take it out for at least six hours following. Then it must be cleansed well with warm soapy water and replaced into its plastic case until the next time you need it."

That sounded incredibly gross. "What method is the best?" I asked.

"No method is completely foolproof, except abstaining. After that, the top three that are suitable for teens are the pill, the patch, or the injection."

There was a pause, and both our eyes trailed to the paper sack I had placed on the desk. "I guess we had better do the test so you can return to school."

I nodded. My eyes followed her over to the metal cabinet where she pulled out a small, white cardboard box. She opened it and took out a flat, plastic thing about five inches by two inches. It looked like a small tray with some paper and plastic over the top. "We call this the reaction unit." She opened my sack and chuckled softly at the sight of the mustard jar.

I watched as she took a couple of drops of my urine from the jar. "Is that all you need?" I asked.

"That's it."

My face flushed. I had brought the jar half full, and Ann only used a couple of drops.

She placed the drops of urine in a receptacle on the reaction unit. She pushed it in and held it as she looked at the clock.

"There is a hormone secreted by pregnant women from the placenta called HCG. This little test adds HCG antibodies to the urine. If there is any HCG present, they will combine with a chemical to turn the line blue. It will look like a plus sign."

"How long do we wait?"

"About another thirty seconds. Two minutes in all."

I rubbed my palms together, then on the legs of my pants. We both stared at the clock as the second hand crept around the dial. My heart moved farther and farther into my throat as it beat faster and faster. Two minutes. An endless length of time. I looked at Ann, afraid to look at the unit in her hand.

"Julie," she said as she placed the reaction unit on the desk. "You are pregnant."

I took a deep breath and looked. A plus sign, dark blue, stood out as clear as could be. There was no doubt.

Ann's voice was soft and understanding. "What do you think you will do about this pregnancy?"

"I . . . I don't know. I guess I never really thought . . ." I looked at her, imploring her for an answer.

Ann sighed, her saddened blue eyes piercing mine. "You are not alone. No one ever thinks it could happen to them. It's hard for a girl to admit she is pregnant." Her tone grew softer. "But you *are.* You must realize the pregnancy will not go away by itself." Her brows scrunched down, crouching over suddenly stern eyes. "Nor will it go away by hiking, running, jumping, or other hard physical activity.

"I wish I could offer you what many call the abortion pill. We don't have it available in our clinic. And abortion is still the surest way to end an unwanted pregnancy at this stage." She paused, probably expecting me to speak, but what could I say? My deepest fear had been handed to me, confirmed by a small, blue plus sign.

Opening a drawer of her desk, she withdrew a pamphlet. She tapped it on the desk as she continued.

"If you want to have an abortion, we can arrange it for you. There are clinics in San Francisco or Oakland that we recommend. But you must remember, the sooner you have an abortion, the safer the procedure will be."

I nodded at intermittent points of her speech, not really hearing anything she said. She placed the pamphlet in my hand as she led me to the door.

"Do you want me to make an appointment for an abortion for you?"

I shook my head. I wanted to get out of this nightmare and back to the real world. If it still existed. "Thanks." I almost couldn't find my voice.

As I went out the door, I passed another young woman, who eyed me. I turned my face, shaking my head to allow a curtain of hair to fall between us.

In the privacy of the car I opened my hand to look at the crumpled pamphlet lying there. The words shouted their message. *Abortion: Every Woman's Choice.* I pored over it, trying to absorb everything it said. I then ripped the evidence into tiny pieces and flung them out the window. I dropped my head onto the steering wheel for a few minutes.

When I looked up, the world had blurred. I wiped underneath my eyes to rid them of smudged makeup. I pushed my hair behind my ear and set my mind to the task of driving.

I arrived at school much later than I had expected. I crept into government, noticing Mr. Silva's stern eye upon me as I took my seat.

The moment class let out, I ran out the door, pretending not to hear Mr. Silva's call: "Miss Marshall, Miss Marshall."

A hazy fog seemed to shroud the day. It must have been my imagination, for the sun warmed everything except my insides. I understood why the girl at the clinic had worn a sweater.

"Are you in there, Julie?" Stephanie tapped her finger on my head.

I shrugged my shoulders and offered her a ride home. I drove in silence as Steph prodded me with questions about my morning's absence.

Finally I spoke. "I woke up with bad cramps. Sorry I didn't call. Hope you didn't wait for me too long."

"No," she replied with a pout. "I'm glad we have a time limit set in case one of us neglects to call the other."

Stephanie's hurt expression showed she sensed the lies. Thankfully she drew her lips in a tight line and said no more.

When I dropped my head on my bed that night, I used the pillow to smother the tears I had been withholding all day. I hoped for sleep and didn't care if I never woke up.

Chapter Eight

I lay on my back, trying to deny the obvious. I sucked in my breath and tried again. No doubt about it, there was something different in there. The round, hard mound rose up from the softness surrounding it. That small mound, just above my pubic bone, must be the alien. The little thing that threatened my sanity, my plans and dreams.

I looked out the window, wanting to curse the sun. It had no right to shine its warmth into my room. For two days I had wanted the sky to cry with me. But no. The sun shone on as though there was nothing wrong with being a teenager, unmarried, and pregnant.

I wanted to call and tell Kyle. Yet every time I picked up the phone, my heart began to beat quickly and hard, seeming to choke my voice. Even if I could speak, what would I say? In my imagination, I told him 23 different ways. Each time I told Kyle in my nicest voice about his impending fatherhood. He, of course, responded by being sweet and having the perfect solution. Whatever that was.

I knew whatever he wanted, I'd do. I wanted more than anything to please him.

I also knew he wouldn't hesitate to drive from The City to see me, showering me with love and kisses. Then we would tell my family together.

So for two days I sat by the phone waiting, waiting . . .

"Hi, hot stuff! What's going on?"

The tension I had kept contained for days suddenly poured out its bitter flavor. "So why haven't you called all week?"

"Sorry," Kyle brushed it off. "I've been making decisions about my future. Where should I apply for college? Should I go out for football or wrestling while I'm there? You know, things like that."

I could feel my dark eyes shooting darts. I pulled on my hair and bristled. "You have another decision to make about your future."

"What's that?"

Then my anger faded. Tears poured down my face. "Kyle," I sobbed. "Kyle . . ."

"Come on, Julie," he said, irritated. "This is costing me money, you know."

Where was the loving concern I had imagined? I began to stammer, "Kyle, I'm . . . I'm . . . pregnant."

The long pause made me shiver. "You're what?"

"You heard," I whispered.

"Unfortunately," he snapped.

"So . . . what are you going to do about it?" I probed.

"What do you mean, what am *I* going to do about it? It's your problem, not mine. Besides, how do I know it's even my brat?"

No words could have hurt me more. "It's yours," I breathed. "I never had sex before you. If you don't believe that, listen to this: I'm probably two months along. That means summer, and you should know summer means you." I stifled a sob.

Kyle's voice became gentle. "I'm sorry. Of course it's mine. You just took me by surprise, that's all."

I asked my question again, desperate for his perfect solution. "So, Kyle, what do we do?"

"Well, there's only one thing *to* do. Get rid of it."

"You mean abortion?"

"Of course."

"I don't know, Kyle. I don't know how I feel about abortion."

"Well, you have no other choice."

"I don't know. I just remember last year, a girl from school named Charlene had an abortion. I was so angry with her that I couldn't speak to her for weeks. All I wanted to do was to walk up to her and grab her arms and shake her till her braces fell out, yelling, 'Charlene! How *could* you?' "

"Oh, Julie. Come off it. Don't you realize things are different when it's you that's pregnant?"

The words cut into my heart. But of course he must be right. Not wanting to, I answered, "Okay."

Then, I needed to know. "Do you love me?"

With zero tenderness, he said, "That's a silly question. Yes. I love you."

"Will you come to see me soon?"

"I guess."

"You don't sound very promising."

"It's up to the old man, Julie. You know that."

"Yeah, right." I didn't believe him for a moment.

"Look, I'll try to convince him, okay?"

"I really need to see you, Kyle."

"Hey, I gotta go."

I possessed neither the strength nor the words with which to protest. I sat there, listening to the click and the final hum of desertion. I pushed the OFF button, hoping to drown out the sounds of emptiness.

Too confused to cry, I stared at the phone, even as it rang again.

In the distance I could hear Tammy's breathless hello, then her feet pounding up the stairs. She banged her fist on my door, calling, "Jan is on the phone!"

"I don't want to talk to her."

"So what'll I tell her?"

"What do I care?"

As Tammy bounded back down the stairs, I changed my mind. I picked up the phone. "Hi, Jan."

Just then Tammy picked up the other phone. "Jan—"

"Thanks, Tammy, I got it." I could envision Tammy's confused expression as she hung up the phone.

"Hi, Julie." Jan spoke gently. "I'm calling to see how you're feeling."

I ignored the unasked questions and asked one of my own. "Jan, why can't my life be like yours?"

"What do you mean, Julie?"

"Why don't you ever fall apart when disaster hits you?"

Jan laughed. "Oh, Julie, you've seen me cry lots of times."

"Yeah, but your tears are different," I insisted. "You're always talking about the good things that come out of rotten situations. Your outlook on everything is so . . . well, it's so different from mine."

"My outlook wasn't always so positive."

"Really? What changed you?" I asked, hoping to find a solution to my world of problems.

"It's Jesus, Julie. He's given me a new outlook on life. The problems are still there, but He gives me the strength to cope with them. Strength to know He has planned for my best even through the hard times."

"Oh, lay off that Jesus stuff. Can't you ever talk without bringing Him up?" I knew I should regret these bitter words, but I didn't.

"I can't quit talking about Jesus any more than I could quit breathing. He is how I live."

"If your stupid Jesus is so good, then why am I pregnant?" I blurted.

I closed my eyes, my anger expressed and shame coming over me. I hadn't wanted to tell Jan. I had just wanted to have the abortion and never let her know. I was sure that now she wouldn't let me baby-sit for her anymore, let alone be my friend.

Jan's soothing voice brought me into a shelter I hadn't known existed. "I thought so. Have you told your mom?"

"No."

"It might be a good idea."

"Why? What can she do?"

"Mothers are a lot more understanding than we give them credit for. Maybe she can help guide your decisions in coping with this."

"I don't need any guidance. I can handle this myself."

"Can you?" Her question pressed into my wounds. "Why don't you come over? It would be easier to talk about it face-to-face."

I had no energy to speak to anyone. I wanted to skip dinner, crawl into bed, and forget this whole nightmare. "Maybe another day. I . . . I just don't feel—"

"That's okay, Julie. Just remember I'm always here to help, to listen, or just to offer a place for you to get away."

"Thanks." She amazed me. I might as well

have slapped her in the face, and still she talked as if I never said what I did about her "friend."

"I'll be praying for you."

Big deal, I wanted to say. Yet the prospect of God knowing about this mess somehow began to make me feel a bit better. "Okay. Bye."

I set the phone back on the table, curled into a ball, and began to plan the next horrid steps of my life.

⊷━━━━⊷

My moist hands shook as I dialed the number. I had to keep wiping them on the bedspread. My foot jiggled as if it had a life of its own.

"Family Planning."

I felt I had lost my voice. "I want to get an abortion."

"How far along do you think you are?"

"I was told probably about seven weeks."

"Are you certain this is what you want?"

"Yes."

"I will need your name and phone number. We will get back to you when we have set up an appointment. Do you prefer going to Oakland or San Francisco?"

"Oakland, I guess."

"We will call you to confirm the appointment tomorrow."

"But you can't call here."

"That's fine. You can call us if you prefer."

I sighed. "Yes."

———

Days continued to pass with extreme effort, as though they might not continue to another sunrise.

The clinic had arranged a procedure date a week from Friday. They suggested I arrange for someone to take me. They said the distance was too great for my emotional condition before the abortion and my physical condition after it.

I would have to tell Mom. I'd thought a lot about it. Yes, it would hurt her. But I figured she would be more hurt to discover later that I hadn't asked for her help. Even if the only help she gave was to drive me to some clinic in Oakland.

Too bad there are no books entitled *How to Tell Your Mom You Are Pregnant*. I could have used one.

Sometimes you needed to wear running shoes and carry a bullhorn to tell Mom anything. When she wasn't at work, she was cleaning. Anytime I approached her, she put me to work at the opposite end of the house.

One day I became desperate. I knew I had to tell her that day, or I might explode like an overblown balloon.

She had wrapped her hair in a red gingham bandanna, and she was waving a can of dust spray in one hand and a cloth in the other. You could see her mind running through her list of things to do as she aimed her body for the kitchen. I jumped in front of her, bracing myself in the doorway. Her eyes searched my face.

"Mom, we really need to talk."

"Sure, Julie," she said, tucking the can and rag under her arm. "Let's sit down for a snack when we get this mess cleaned up." She pulled my hands down from the door frame, stuffing them with the spray can and rag. "Go dust the upstairs, would you please? Thanks. I won't forget the snack. We can have ice cream."

She eased by me as I numbly said, "Sure, Mom." I knew that when we finished housecleaning, it would be dinnertime. That would be rushed, too, for it was her and Dad's special night out.

My final approach would be tactless and painful, but she left me no alternative. It would have to be after they came home.

I thought I'd die before they came home. I was sitting on the sofa when I heard the garage door open. I took a deep breath and tried in vain to sit still. I folded my hands, feeling like the bad little girl trying to fool her parents into thinking she was good simply by looking the part. Dad walked in, said his usual gruff hello, and kissed me on the cheek. He sauntered upstairs to bed. I grabbed Mom's wrist. "Can we please talk, *now?*"

I could see by the look on her face that I'd

gotten through. She sat down, and I wiped my palms on my jeans.

"Mom, remember all the teasing about me getting fat?"

She nodded and jumped to her usual conclusions. "I'm sorry, Julie. We all love you and don't mean to hurt your feelings."

I shook my head in frustration, letting my hair sting my cheeks. "No, Mom, you don't understand. You're right. I *am* getting fat. Most girls do when they're pregnant."

Her expression turned to disbelief. As tears came to my eyes, she must have realized this was no cute little joke. She scanned me, searching for proof. She burst into tears, putting her head into her hands.

"Mom." I grabbed her arm, trying to pull her hands from her face. "Please don't cry."

"Julie Marie, leave me alone. I don't want to talk." She stumbled up the stairs, leaving me to stare at the telephone commercial on TV.

I sat there wondering if my heart was still beating. My muscles had frozen, and so had everything else. Maybe 20 minutes had passed when I forced myself off the couch to turn off the TV.

When I reached my room, I sat staring in the mirror. This had to be happening to someone else. But the person in the mirror looked like a frightened me.

I could hear muffled sobs and occasional voices drifting through the hallway.

Crawling into bed, I pulled my pillow tight over my ears. I bit my lip, trying desperately not to cry.

Slowly a new fear crept inside me. The fear that tomorrow would come.

Chapter Nine

I woke as Mom lowered herself onto the edge of my bed. "Julie," she said softly, touching my shoulder. "Can we talk now?"

I looked at her, turning away when I saw her red-rimmed eyes. Her lids were swollen from crying. "Sure, Mom," I said, frightened by what she might have to say.

"Honey, I'm sorry I couldn't talk to you last night." Her hand dropped from my shoulder to clasp her other tissue-filled hand. "I . . . I wanted to think more about what you had said."

"I don't understand." I plucked at the sheet.

"Can I be honest?"

"I suppose." *Now why would I want her to lie?*

"I never thought I would be sitting here with you, discussing something like this."

I looked away, ashamed.

"I guess I never thought I would see you in this situation, and that's why I never discussed . . . umm . . . sex before."

I felt as though I were being stripped naked in front of her. Her obvious embarrassment joined mine to make us both uneasy.

"At first I was angry with you. 'What a little tramp,' I thought."

"Mom!" I protested, now facing her.

"Wait, Julie. Then I remembered the relationship your father and I had before we were married. I tried to remember how much I loved him and the way I didn't think much about our actions."

I tried not to look shocked. I had hardly ever thought of Mom and Dad as doing anything more than kissing. I guess that's because that's all we kids ever saw.

"I should have thought about those feelings before," she continued with difficulty. "We never, uh . . . well, I never could have gotten pregnant, but if our engagement had been much longer . . . well, who can say?"

She shook her head as if bringing herself in from a daydream. "I should have talked about sex with you. I should have told you how to prevent babies."

I gave her a slight nod. A little information like I received at the Family Planning Clinic would have helped a lot.

"So after I blamed you, I shifted the blame to myself."

That sounds pretty good, I thought. *Maybe this isn't really my fault after all.*

Mom's sharp words caught my attention. "But

I'm not to blame, Julie. You made the decision to have sex with Kyle. I didn't force you to."

My eyes brimmed with tears.

"After a while I blamed Kyle," she continued. "I told myself, 'It must be his fault. He forced Julie into this.'"

"Mom, no one forced me into anything."

She sighed. "I know." Her voice trailed off. "Julie, we all bear some blame. We share the guilt. Me, for not guiding you as a mother should. And you—"

"But Mom, I didn't think I could get pregnant." At that moment I realized how absurd that statement was.

We both said nothing for a moment, then Mom looked toward the door and pleaded, "Why, Julie, why?"

"Mom, I'm sorry." Another dumb statement. I was so confused, I didn't know whether I was sorry or not. I didn't know if I was alive or not. I didn't know anything.

Mom interrupted my thoughts. "Over and over I thought that, no matter what, I love you. Because I love you, I must stand with you, not hide in a corner, not point an accusing finger at anyone."

"Oh, Mom, I love you, too," I blurted. We both burst into fresh tears and gave each other a hug that would have crushed a bear.

Wiping her eyes, Mom said, "What are you going to do?"

I enunciated each word in my attempt not to stammer, "I have an appointment for an abortion."

Mom gulped, and I could tell she did not want to face reality any more than I did. "When?"

"Friday."

"So soon," she said to herself.

I spoke with borrowed authority and confidence. "The sooner the better, and safer," I quoted.

She just looked at me, her reddened eyes full of pain. And perhaps fear?

"Mom, I have to go to Oakland for the abortion. Will you take me?"

She gulped again. "I don't know if I approve of abortion."

I looked at her, not knowing what to say.

As Mom looked into my begging eyes, she said, her voice shaking, "I will take you. I disagree with your choice, but I will honor your right to make it." She shuddered. "I hope your father understands."

"Will you tell him for me please, Mama?"

I hadn't called her Mama in years. I bet she understood why I used that special name now. And so she became willing to ease my pain, if only a bit, by telling Dad about my unpopular decision.

I avoided Dad all day. At dinner he could hardly say hello to me. Before being seated, he gave

Tammy her customary kiss, and Mom hers. He didn't attempt to complete the tradition I used to hate—to give me one, too.

I missed that kiss, but I understood. I would never again be his little girl. I knew he accepted what had happened but wouldn't talk about it. That's just the way Dad was.

I went to bed early, wanting to avoid all family contact. Even if they didn't cut me off, I had to separate myself. I no longer felt like a part of this respectable family.

It was so strange. Just a few short weeks ago, I had complained to Jan about how unloving our family was. And now I saw that wasn't true. The love had always been there; I just hadn't seen it.

I tried not to think about what would happen in only a few days. My body would be altered, not to mention my life. But I hoped there would be less alteration than if I carried this alien for another seven months. I wanted to be parted from it as soon as possible.

The easy way out. Not even Stephanie would have to know.

Chapter Ten

"Is this it, Mom?"

"Yes. Are you sure you don't want me to come in?"

I took a deep breath and lied. "No. Don't come in. I'll be all right."

"I'll come for you in three hours."

"Okay."

She stuffed some money into my hand. "It's building E-6."

"Thanks." I turned and began to open the door.

"Julie."

I swung around to face her. "What?"

She wiped tears from her eyes, hesitating. "Bye."

I was pretty sure there had been something more she wanted to say, but she was unable to speak. As she drove away, I felt a sense of loss. A loss of what, I'm not sure.

A fairly large office complex sat in front of me. I don't know why I had expected a sleazy, run-down, back-alley house. I wound around the wooden buildings, set among lush, green landscaping. I found E-6 between a dentist's office and a chiropractor's office.

As I pushed open the glass door, a scene of contrasts appeared before me.

The large waiting room had tastefully papered walls decorated with sketches of beautiful, modern women. Soft music filled the air. Couches and chairs lined the walls. Comfortable. Peaceful. But not.

People were strewn about. Some male, some female. All waiting. Fear painted the women's faces. Some with shame. The men looked sad, uncomfortable, and sometimes a touch angry. No one spoke.

Next to the door, a man draped his slumbering form across a chair. He folded his arms across his chest, reminiscent of my father before the TV, "watching" football games.

A young girl, maybe even younger than I, rocked back and forth on a chair. She bit one fingernail, her eyes round with emotion. Along with fear and shame, I detected confusion. I wanted to reach out and touch her, but I could barely keep myself together.

As I approached the reception window, a door opened and an attendant called a name. An older woman rose from a couch. Her long, stringy, gray-streaked hair draped about her face.

"Can I help you?" a friendly voice questioned.

I turned to the receptionist. "My name is Julie Marshall. I have an 11 o'clock appointment."

"I have some papers for you to fill out, Julie.

Fill in this upper portion here, read these two blue papers, and sign the yellow one stating you have read them."

I nodded as the pleasant young woman handed me three pieces of paper, a clipboard, and a pen. I tried to focus my eyes and understanding on the sheet of instructions, which told what would be happening to me during the next two and a half hours. Nothing penetrated the nervous glaze that covered my mind. I gave up and signed the papers, returning them to the receptionist.

"That will be $325, please."

I handed her the cash my mom had given me.

"Would you like something to help you relax?" she asked.

I nodded and she handed me a paper cup of water and a small pill.

I returned to my seat and began to check out what type of woman would seek an abortion. Some were beautiful, some looked like well-used pieces of equipment. Some heavy, some slender. It was hard to believe each had something in common. Their bodies all harbored an unwanted alien. And nobody wanted that alien to become a person to complicate their lives.

The realization eased through me that I was there for the same reason and purpose.

Suddenly I felt I was drowning in fear. Wave after wave enveloped me. I felt I was fighting for a breath. Even though my eyes were open wide, I could see everything only through a misty haze. Shapes had little color, no names, and dull voices. I gripped the seat of the armless chair and held on.

I bit my bottom lip and squeezed my eyes shut. Time wore snails' feet. The only thing that penetrated this awesome fear was someone speaking my name.

Somehow I got off the chair and walked toward the voice. I didn't care who the voice belonged to, I just went.

The woman led me down a hallway past many doors. She paused and opened a door, letting me into a bright, clean room. It was furnished with a sink, work counter, refrigerator, and a couple of chairs. Various equipment, test tubes, and timers lay about the counter. It looked like a lab. A young, attractive woman looked up from her work and greeted me. "Hi, Julie. I'm the lab technician."

I tried very hard to smile, with no success. "Hi."

"Take this cup and give us a small sample of your urine for a pregnancy test, please."

I nodded as I took the paper cup from her outstretched hand.

It only took a couple of minutes for me to complete my task. My hand shook as I returned the cup to the lab technician. She weighed me, then took my temperature, blood pressure, and pulse rate. Then, the procedure I hated: drawing blood. "What's the blood for?"

"We do a few quick tests on it. Hematocrit, hemoglobin, and Rh factor. If you are Rh negative, we will give you a RhoGAM injection following the procedure."

I nodded as if I knew what she was talking about.

She took me down another hallway to a room. It had four cubicles with bright sky blue drapes hanging in front of the doorways to offer privacy. Three women dressed in paper gowns sat staring at a table between them. It seemed odd that no one was reading the magazines lying there. Each woman looked up briefly as I entered the room.

"Go into one of the cubicles and remove your clothes. You may leave your socks on, but everything else must come off."

I glanced at the dark-haired, brown-eyed lady who had led me here. "Why everything?"

"The physician will want to do a breast check before he begins the procedure."

I cringed. No one but Kyle had ever touched my breasts.

"Put your clothes into the small plastic bag you will find in the cubicle," she continued. "You will carry the bag with you throughout your stay here until it is time to put your clothes back on."

I entered the cubicle nearest the door. I

undressed as slowly as possible, not enjoying the thought of putting on the paper gown. I hate those awful things. I don't understand why the manufacturers insist on leaving in the breeze that seems to come with them.

I picked up a magazine before I sat down in the cold chair. A few minutes had passed when a girl who looked a couple of years older than I approached the entrance to the room. Her escort gave her the same undressing instructions, and the girl nodded with what appeared to be impatience.

After shedding her clothes and putting on a gown, she sat next to me. She had fastened the front of her ash blonde hair back with a clip at the crown of her head. Her blue eyes were confident, unlike any of the others in the small room.

She leaned over to me and said, "Hi, my name is Rachel. What's yours?"

"Julie."

"This your first time here?"

I nodded.

"This is my second."

I tried in vain to conceal my shock. Someone would actually go through this more than once?

"Hey, you scared?"

I nodded again.

"Don't be. There's nothin' to it. The worst part is lying on one of those awful tables with your legs spread apart."

"Doesn't it hurt?" I whispered.

"Nah. Not really. It just feels a little like cramps when you get your period."

"What about that machine. Doesn't it hurt?"

"Of course not. By then it's almost over. It feels a little like something's being sucked out of you. But big deal. That's what's happening anyway."

"What about after you get home?"

"I felt fine. I bled for a few days. Life returned to normal." She looked down at her stomach. "At least for a while, anyway."

I knew Rachel was trying to be helpful, but instead of soothing my fears, she caused them to grow.

"Your boyfriend know you're here?" Rachel asked, unwrapping a piece of gum.

"Yes."

"What does he think?"

"He's the one who suggested it."

"Of course. They all do."

Offended by her obvious slander of Kyle's reputation, I snapped, "He loves me and wants the best for me."

"Sure, honey, that's why he's here holding your hand."

I opened my mouth twice, but I couldn't think of a good comeback.

"Look," Rachel said, giving my arm a swift pat, "I don't mean to talk nasty about your man. I seem to spit all my venom for my man on everyone else's. But I'm surprised you didn't think of the abortion first."

"I guess because I've never liked the thought of abortion."

She looked amazed. "Then why're you here?"

"Because," I said hesitating, "my boyfriend wanted it."

She pulled her brows together and scratched her head under the hair clip. Now I had left her speechless.

I clasped my hands together, dropped my chin to my chest, and closed my eyes. I didn't want to talk anymore. I wanted to think, but that was so hard to do.

Why *was* I there? Whose choice was this abortion anyway? No matter how I looked at it, the choice was Kyle's. I hadn't thought much about anything except, *Why am I pregnant?*

Thinking was too hard right now. As long as I was there, I figured I might as well go through with it.

An attendant called another name, and I realized I was next. My heart skipped a beat, then began to race, and I froze. I suppose if someone were there to take a picture of me right then and show it around, folks would think a corpse had been lifted from its casket and propped in a chair.

"This is no mannequin," I could almost hear some-one say. "Mannequin faces never show absolute ter-ror such as this."

A woman in a marine blue cotton gown broke into my morbid daydream. "Julie," she said.

I paused, then stood. The floor felt so cold under my feet. I had forgotten to leave my socks on. Numb, I picked up the plastic bag filled with my clothes.

My insides quivered like Jell-O as I walked down the hall after her. I followed her through a door marked OR. I scanned the room. A counter-top and metal sink lined one wall. A bed on wheels fitted with a paper sheet and a pillow sat against the wall on the opposite side of the room. They called the bed a gurney.

In the center of the room was a strange-looking table. It was cushioned and covered with paper. The strange part about it was the size. It was short. Too short for anyone I knew, unless we were dis-cussing eight-year-olds. Two metal arms with cupped fingerless hands at the end of them extended from each side of the lower end of the table. Each stretched out and up into the air, spreading widely apart.

Beside the table on one side was a thing that looked like a cabinet on wheels. There were two jars and a plastic hose sticking out of the top.

Next to the cabinet was a metal tray, also on wheels. Placed neatly upon it was a row of instruments. Long metal rods that gradually got bigger caught my eye.

"Up on the table, Julie," the nurse chirped. At that I burst into tears.

The nurse put her arm around me and helped me to sit on the small stool at the foot of the examining table. She brushed the hair from my face. "Julie, are you sure you want to go through with this?"

I could only cry. I couldn't think.

The door opened, and a bearded man walked in. I tried to draw into myself, afraid of his reaction to my tears.

He approached me, placing a hand on my shoulder. "What's wrong?"

I shrugged, trying to suck in my tears, but only making a nasty sound.

"Are you scared?"

I nodded. But it was more than that. Much more. I wasn't sure I believed abortion was okay. I wasn't sure that this was the right choice. I wasn't sure of anything except I was here, I was alone, and Kyle didn't care.

"You aren't sure about this?"

I shook my head, looking at him, my arms wrapped around my waist. I hoped he could somehow read in my eyes what I couldn't say.

"Get up on the examining table, and we'll see how far along you are."

I obeyed. I understood what Rachel meant about the embarrassment of lying with my legs spread apart on that table. My buttocks were all the way down at the edge of the table. My legs, high in the air, were supported under my knees by the metal "pipes." My ankles rested in the cupped hands.

The doctor washed, then slipped surgical gloves onto his hands and reached what felt like his whole hand into my vagina. I gasped. It hurt. He told me to relax. If I hadn't been so scared, I probably would have laughed. RELAX? Funny man! How could anyone relax with a stranger's hand inside of her?

I tried to think of something else. Something nice. Our last vacation. Christmas. My birthday. Nothing worked. Rivulets of tears flowed from the corners of my eyes and puddled in my ears.

The doctor pressed his hand on my stomach as he moved his right hand gently about inside me. He turned to the nurse and said, "Nine weeks."

He looked at me and said, "Julie, we don't need to do the procedure today. You aren't emotionally ready to make this decision. You still have three more weeks in which this can be done safely. Go home. Think about it. If you feel you are ready to try again, give us a call."

He slipped off the gloves, tossed them into the

trash, then patted me on the leg. He washed his hands at the sink and left.

The nurse helped me up and handed me some tissues and my bag of clothes. "Julie, you're on your own now. I must get ready for the next patient."

As I left the OR, I glanced into a room I hadn't noticed on my earlier trip down the hall.

A small sign marked Recovery was posted on the wall beside the door. Inside, a row of gurneys lined the far, windowless wall. A woman draped with a paper sheet occupied each one. All the women were silent. Shock had replaced fear. The alien had been pulled from them. Mine still remained.

An eerie feeling passed over me, and I shuddered. I increased my pace to reach the room of cubicles once more.

Rachel was gone, but I didn't really care. I changed more quickly this time. I was anxious to leave.

The kind receptionist returned my money. I walked out into the bright sunshine and sat under a tree. I wished I hadn't insisted Mom go shopping instead of waiting at the clinic.

Uncontrolled sobs overwhelmed me, and I hugged my knees for comfort. *Oh, God, I'm so confused,* I thought. *What am I going to do? Oh, God. Help me! What am I going to do?*

Chapter Eleven

"Forget it, Julie. Forget it. It's all over."

"But, Kyle!" I pleaded through my tears.

"Look, honey. I told you to get an abortion. If you can't even follow a basic instruction, our relationship is over."

"I love you."

"If you loved me, you would have gotten that abortion."

"I thought you loved me."

"I thought I did, too. I guess we were both mistaken."

"Kyle, I need your help."

"Okay. I'll send you $250. That's what I was going to send you for the abortion anyway."

I pulled hard on the hair twisted around my finger. "Not that kind of help, Kyle. I need *you.*"

"I already told you no, Julie. I've had enough. I want my life to go on without any hassles. And it's obvious you are becoming a big one."

Anger swelled my heart. "What about *my* future, Kyle? Don't you think I'll be hassled?"

"That's your own tough luck. You seem to think our relationship was more than a casual summer romance."

"Wasn't it?" I whispered.

Kyle scoffed. "Chicks. You all think a guy paying a little attention to you means something."

My jaw dropped. "But if you're having sex that means the relationship is very important to both people."

"I told you, sex is just like ice cream. It's something to enjoy. We've enjoyed our ice cream and now it might be time to try a different flavor."

I felt like I did when the planes slammed into the World Trade Center. Stunned. Shocked. Disbelieving. "You can't—"

"Look, hot stuff. We had a good time this summer. But it's time to move on. I don't want to hear from you again. Understand?"

A flame of anger shot from some mother-grizzly place inside me. For once I wanted to have the last word. "No, I don't understand. And you *will* hear from me again. Good-bye!" I punched the OFF button, wishing I'd slammed the phone on the table first.

I declined dinner and had tears instead. I didn't understand why my life had to suck so badly. Emotions spun around inside me like the lottery balls before they're spit out of the machine. I didn't know which consumed me more—the raging anger or the heart-ripping hurt.

"God, why don't You do something?" I shouted at the ceiling.

When the tears stopped, I paced like a caged cat. Anxious, restless. The emotional energy gaining momentum until I thought I might explode.

I picked up the phone. I needed help. I needed to talk to someone, someone who loved me.

Jan's line rang until the machine picked up.

I hung up and dialed another number. "Is Stephanie there, please?"

I twirled my hair into a perfect ringlet while I waited.

"Yes," Stephanie said, breathless.

"It's me. Julie. Can you talk?"

"Yeah, sure, Jule. What's up?"

"I've got to tell you, Steph." I began to cry again.

"Hey, Jule, what is it?"

"You've got to promise you won't tell a soul."

"You know I won't, Julie."

"Kyle has broken up with me." Sobs almost concealed my voice.

Stephanie hesitated a moment. "Maybe that's for the best, Julie."

"What do you mean?" I almost screamed. "Some friend and comfort you are."

"I'm sorry, Julie. It's just . . . well, I never thought Kyle was real good for you."

"Oh, what do you know?"

She didn't answer.

"Hey, Stephanie. Look. I'm hurting so bad right now—"

"I bet." After a pause she forced some cheerfulness. "Hey, why don't we go shopping tomorrow?"

"Can't. I have a doctor's appointment."

"Oh, yeah? What for?"

I clenched my teeth, closed my eyes, and wondered what I should say.

Stephanie spoke up again. "Which doctor?"

"Dr. Womack."

"I've never heard of him. What kind of doctor is he?"

"An obstetrician."

"A what?"

"A doctor who takes care of pregnant women." I paused and took a deep breath. "I'm pregnant, Steph."

I heard her gasp and felt myself suddenly grow weak. "Oh, Julie. I'm so sorry. What are you going to do?"

"Go to the doctor's tomorrow."

"Don't be funny. What are you going to do with the baby?"

"I don't know yet."

"Does Kyle know?"

"Why do you think he's breaking up with me?"

"Oh." I could almost see Stephanie fidgeting. I felt it over the phone. Suddenly she said, "Julie, my mom's calling. I'll call you later."

"Okay. Bye." Some help she was. What happened when I needed friends the most? Everyone split. So who was I supposed to turn to? Who could keep me from collapsing?

"——"

Dr. Bowers. Dr. Fetler. Dr. Womack. Obstetrician/ Gynecologist Group.

I pulled open the door and let Mom walk in first. She went to the reception window and announced my name. The woman handed her a clipboard with a pen on a ball-chain leash. I felt so dumb. Like a little kid in a doctor's office who couldn't fend for herself.

Mom chose a seat. I plopped myself down next to a woman in obvious discomfort. She used her bloated stomach as a tray, resting her crossed arms on it.

Muzak played over the speakers, and I heard an instrumental version of an old Madonna song. Not my style. I leaned to complain to Mom, and what was she doing? She was filling out the sheet of paper for me. "Mom, I can do that, thank you. I'm a big girl now."

Mom looked hurt and embarrassed. "I'm sorry, Julie. I wasn't thinking."

She handed me the board with the pen trailing along behind. I got halfway through and had to ask her for some of the answers anyway. They asked who would pay for the bill, the address of Dad's work, and so on.

We were lucky, Mom said, that Dad's insurance would help pay for this pregnancy.

I let Mom return the form to the window, while I pretended to read a magazine. My eyes couldn't focus on the words. All the pregnant women in the large room were far more interesting. I had never in my life seen so many stomachs in various stages of swelling.

I tried to imagine what the women used to look like before their bodies became so disfigured. Then I wondered what I would look like in the future.

Maybe I should have gotten the abortion after all. Did I really want my body to be stretched out of shape like these bodies here?

I was glad they summoned me as Julie Marshall. Not Mrs. Marshall, or worse, Miss Marshall.

Thankful that Mom didn't try to come with me, I self-consciously walked across the room and stepped through the doorway.

The nurse led me to the scale. Her pointed chin, her glasses, and her hair poked into a bun brought to mind an old fairy tale. Hansel and Gretel?

As I stepped on the scale, I wished I had worn my lighter-weight clothes instead of jeans, boots, and a heavy sweater.

She pushed a paper cup into my hand. I wondered if I would ever get over the embarrassment of handing someone a cup full of my urine. Just then, she informed me that from then on, I would need to produce a sample at each of my appointments.

When I finished, she led me to a small, windowless room. One wall had a sink nestled in a countertop. The opposite wall had a door in the center of it.

Just like at the abortion clinic, a funny-looking short table sat in the center of the room. A wheeled stool and a gooseneck floor lamp were at the foot of the exam table.

The nurse told me to undress in the dressing room, pointing her chin and finger toward a curtain. The tiny cubby made me wonder how fat women dressed in there. Or pregnant women. I put my clothes on the bench attached to the wall, trying to avoid looking at myself in the full-length mirror hanging on the wall over the bench.

Once again, a breezy gown took the place of my clothes. I peeked through the curtain. The nurse stood there looking impatient.

She patted the table. "Sit here, please."

As I sat, my naked behind stuck to the paper. The nurse put a sheet on my lap.

She checked my blood pressure and pulse. "And why are we here today, Julie?"

"I'm pregnant," I answered, matching her innocent tone.

"Oh? And when was your last menstrual period?"

I got the impression she didn't believe me. "July eleventh."

Her eyebrows rose again as she checked her chart. No doubt to see how old I was, or rather, how young.

I wanted to stick my tongue out at her when she wasn't looking.

After she bustled out the door, I wanted to snoop around the stuff on the counter. But I was afraid to get off the table. Afraid the paper would stick to my backside and trail behind me like toilet tissue on the bottom of a shoe. Afraid the doctor would catch me with my gown open wide in the back, looking at his things.

I leaned way over, trying to see the interesting gadgets and booklets from my perch. The biggest curiosity was a large, see-through plastic thing with something pink in the middle of it. I supposed it was a uterus. It looked kind of like the pictures they showed us in health class last year.

Instead of being a snoop, I waited in this freezing room forever, or at least 12 hours, before the doctor finally showed up.

In the meantime, I memorized his little framed documents posted around the room learning all the details of his medical schooling. I felt someone could have put something a little more interesting to look at on the walls.

A form came flying into the room with a white coat trailing behind like angels' wings.

"Well, good afternoon, Julie. I'm Dr. Womack. What can I do for you?"

His cheeriness threw me. After the nurse, I expected an old grouch. His balding head reminded me of a bulging abdomen—and the reason I was there. "I'm pregnant," I said.

"Well, so you are. When was your last menstrual period?"

I got the feeling he and his nurse ought to get together or that he should have read the chart. "July eleventh."

"How are you feeling?"

"Fine, I guess."

"Good."

It was funny how during the whole time he made small talk, he had me lie down and began to feel my breasts with icy hands. His chatter helped me to keep my mind off the total embarrassment.

"Okay, Julie. It's time to take a look." He pushed a button and said into a speaker, "Pam, room three, please."

"Oh, no!" I wanted to say. "Do you have to?" The doctor was okay, but that nurse?

The door opened and a young woman entered.

Her brown hair, the same color as mine, curled about her face. "Hi," she said, her eyes cheerful behind her glasses.

"This here's Julie," the doctor said to the nurse.

"Hi, Julie. I'm Pam."

"Hi."

"Julie, you need to scoot all the way down to the bottom of the table so Doctor can examine you."

Eager to please them both, I scooted down, almost too far.

The doctor picked up a thing that looked like a cross between a metal duckbill and a clamp. "What's that?"

Dr. Womack laughed. "This here cold thing is called a speculum. It opens up your vagina so I can get a good look at your cervix. The cervix is the neck of your womb, which sticks out into your vagina."

"You're right, it *is* cold," I said as he put it in. "Isn't anything warm in this office?"

"Hey, Pam, looks like we've got a sassy one here." Pam gave me a wink. "Okay now, Julie," the doctor continued in a serious tone. "I am going to take a mucous sample from your cervix for what is called a Pap smear."

"A Pap smear?" I questioned.

"It's a simple test to check for cervical cancer."

"You don't think I have cancer, do you?"

"Probably not. But I can't know unless I do the test."

"Aren't I too young to have that kind of cancer?" It sounded so much like a woman's disease, and I certainly didn't feel like a woman.

"No, you are not too young. The younger you start sexual intercourse and the more partners you have, the greater your chance of developing this type of cancer. Last year we had a 15-year-old girl in the first stages of the disease."

"Oh."

By now the doctor had removed the duckbill thing he called a speculum and had put in his gloved hand and was feeling around. Knowing what to expect helped me to be a bit more calm and not to gasp as loudly as I had at the abortion clinic.

"I highly recommend you have an HIV test," he stated as he poked and prodded.

"Dr. Womack, I don't think AIDS—"

Dr. Womack held up his other hand to silence me. "Young lady, no one who has sex is immune to AIDS. Especially those without a committed partner. I will order one for you."

I closed my mouth. No one believed me that Kyle couldn't have AIDS. I started to wonder if I was the one who was all wrong. *Oh, God,* I prayed as panic nudged me, *don't let that happen too.*

Dr. Womack brought me out of my panicked thoughts. "Well, Julie, you are just about three months pregnant. I want you to dress and meet me in my office so I can give you some instructions."

Dr. Womack's office looked just like his personality. A plastic cube of pictures sat on his desk. It had various pictures of children, a woman, and himself. A fancy electronic spinning top waited on a pedestal to be charged and spun. A couple of Lego Star Wars figures stood at battle ready.

A brown globe with old, ancient-looking writing on it perched on a pedestal next to the desk. I hadn't quite finished reading all the medical titles on his books when he came in.

The minute the door opened, he began talking.

"Julie, many girls your age don't want to admit they're pregnant until quite late in the pregnancy. You did the right thing by coming in early. Both you and the baby will benefit as a result.

"However, the honest facts are: You're still a youngster, and your body hasn't finished the job of growing and developing itself. So it's of vital importance for you to eat well and take the vitamins I'm prescribing for you. The baby will benefit and so will you.

"Whenever you eat, I want you to remember you are feeding your baby the same thing. Cokes, Krispy Kremes, French fries, and candy bars are fine once in a while, but they don't give you or your baby the nutrition you both need to grow properly. You want your child to have a good chance in life and to be intelligent. Good nutrition on your part will help before your child is born.

"Eat three good meals a day or five to six snack-type meals. Some good snacks would be cheese, fruit, unsalted nuts, raw vegetables, or yogurt. Drink lots of liquids, like milk, juices, and water. Any questions?"

My head whirled from the amount of facts this doctor poured out in such a small amount of time. "No, I guess not."

"Next time before you come, write down any questions you have on a piece of paper. That way you won't forget any if you become flustered here in the office."

His hand flew as he wrote on a couple of pieces of paper. "Here's your prescription for prenatal vitamins and a lab request slip."

He ripped both pages off their tablets and handed them to me. "Go to the lab at the hospital next door, and they will phone the results of the tests to me."

I looked at the lab slip with dismay. "I have two questions now."

"Okay. Shoot."

"What does prenatal mean?"

"Before birth. Next?"

Holding up the lab slip, I asked, "Why do you need blood?"

"We do a set of five tests to check for syphilis,

anemia, your blood type and factor, and to see if you are immune to German measles. We've also requested the AIDS test."

I nodded, knowing the lab slip sealed my fate. The blood must come out.

"Julie, one more thing. I don't usually discuss finances with my patients, but you are a special case. Are your parents able to cover the cost of your prenatal care?"

"Well," I hesitated, "Mom said Dad's insurance will cover most of it."

"That's good. If there is ever any problem, let me know. Then we can refer you to Medi-Cal for either cost sharing or total coverage.

"Also, I am going to recommend you to a Department of Health program. It's called Women, Infants and Children—WIC for short. There they will give you some coupons for food supplements that will help you to maintain the nutritional standards we spoke of earlier."

"I think Mom will appreciate that," I said. "I've been eating everything but the furniture. She's been complaining about her enormous food bill."

Dr. Womack nodded as he listened, filling out a blue referral slip and then signing it.

"Okay, Julie. We'll see you in a month."

"Thanks, Dr. Womack."

Chapter Twelve

····——————··

My second trip to Dr. Womack's office wasn't bad at all. Probably because this time I didn't have to take my clothes off. He just talked a lot about my health and the baby. When he got to the part about sex during pregnancy and Kyle and my choices for the baby, I did a lot of nodding and shrugging. I fiddled with the metal toy on his desk. I didn't want to hear what he had to say, didn't want to deal with it.

After I made my next appointment, I thought about how it might be almost fun coming to the doctor's. I felt the people here understood me. They were the only ones I felt free to talk to about being pregnant.

I was embarrassed around Mom. I didn't know whether I should act like a daughter or a guest.

I'd been avoiding Jan. She'd always been so nice about everything. She'd always been there for me. But it scared me to think that maybe she'd changed her mind now. I didn't want to give her the chance to say she didn't want me around anymore. I couldn't take added rejection. Especially from her.

And Stephanie? What a joke. She treated me like I was fragile or something. She was also late to school almost every day. I was sure it was so she didn't have to walk with me. I really didn't blame her. I felt as awkward as she did about it.

There wasn't much to talk about now anyway. We couldn't talk about the boys she was dating because I felt funny and left out.

We couldn't talk about Baby because that brought up the subject of sex.

"So is it fun?" Stephanie asked one day.

"Is what fun?"

"You know . . . being with a guy . . . like that."

She was worse than Mom. She couldn't say *sex*, either. "It was weird."

"Then why did you?"

How could I explain how physically it could be good, but emotionally it might not, and it made it all messed up inside? The conflicting parts tore at each other.

"I don't know," I said, thinking she'd let me talk it through so maybe I could understand better. "I hoped it would be just like ice cream."

"Just like ice cream?"

"You know, something great and wonderful."

She still looked awfully confused, and I could see the question again forming on her lips. "Ice cream?"

"Oh, forget it."

We walked the rest of the way to school in silence.

On my third visit to the doctor's, they weighed me, took my urine sample, and checked my blood pressure and pulse. It felt strange to sit fully clothed on the exam table as I waited for Dr. Womack.

The minute he flew into the room, his mouth began to flap like his trailing coat. "Hi, Julie. Good to see you looking so well. I hope you are eating well, also. Not overdoing the salt or sugars, I hope. How about soft drinks? Not more than once in a while, please."

Meanwhile, he had me lift my dress to my belly button and lie down. He pulled out a round metal thing from his pocket.

"What are you going to do, build a house?" I asked, pointing to the measuring-tape canister.

"No, but you are building a baby, and I want to see how construction is going." He put one end of the measuring tape on the top of my pubic bone. The other end he held in place on my belly after he had poked around a while. "This is part of your prenatal care routine. I will always measure your uterus to see how much it grows from one visit to the next."

He turned, flipped a switch on a machine behind him. Turning back, he held a bottle of goo in one hand and something that looked like a microphone in the other. He grinned. "This is my favorite part."

"What?"

He squirted some of the cold goo low on my belly, then touched the microphone to the goo. He moved it around, his face wearing a thoughtful, searching expression. Suddenly, I heard a rapid thumping, like a fast heartbeat.

"There it is," he breathed.

My voice caught in my throat. After a long moment, I could speak again. "The baby?"

He nodded. "A very healthy baby."

I lay there listening, trying to knit this undeniable reality with my desire to pretend it wasn't real. I closed my eyes. Incorporating the baby's heartbeat into my heart. No longer an alien. A baby.

The beat abruptly stopped.

My eyes flew open, my own heart racing. Dr. Womack faced the machine, wiping off the microphone with a paper towel. I breathed again.

"I'll have the nurse check your insurance to see if you're covered for an ultrasound." He turned and patted my ankle. "You can sit up now."

"Sometime around the end of this month, middle of December, you ought to be able to feel the baby move. And if your insurance allows for an ultrasound you'll probably know if it's a boy or a girl."

I suppose this is stupid for most women who got pregnant on purpose—but I wasn't sure I wanted to know. Hearing the heartbeat threw me one unexpected curve. I didn't know if I wanted to know more about this creature inside.

"Any questions?"

"Only one," I said, sure it was a stupid question.

"Only one?"

"Yeah. Is it okay to sleep on my stomach?"

"It's getting uncomfortable, isn't it?"

"Yes."

"It won't hurt the baby any. As time goes along it would be best for you to get used to sleeping on your left side."

"Okay."

"See you in December. Remember to eat well! You want to build a good, healthy baby."

"Right," I replied with no great conviction.

———

Mr. Silva was getting on my nerves. His incessant monotone was enough to drive anyone to the daydreaming ditch.

At least I wasn't the only one who felt this way. Tom, the class clown, mimicked Mr. Silva. David made his best paper airplanes. But the teacher seemed totally oblivious to the passing of notes, chitchat, and hidden giggles.

I didn't join the pranks anymore. I huddled in my coat, using the chill of December as an excuse to hide the changes going on in my body. I slipped into daydreams until I didn't even notice the rest of the class.

I daydreamed about Baby. Always Baby. Ever since I felt the flutter and tap of its first movements the fourth day of this month, Baby was light in my womb but heavy on my mind.

The moment I felt the baby move it became even more real. It burrowed itself deep inside me, going to a place I couldn't find words to express. The more it fluttered and tunneled, the less I knew what to say—and the more I withdrew into myself.

Now that I couldn't deny its existence, what was I going to do with it? I couldn't pretend it would just disappear.

I didn't want an ultrasound. I'm so thankful Dad's insurance didn't cover it. I didn't want to know what it was. I didn't want to get attached.

I wondered what it would look like. I'd never thought babies looked like much of anything. Would this one be different?

Would I have to drop out of school? That might be kind of nice to avoid boring teachers like Mr. Silva. But what would I do with myself that would be less boring?

In PE I'd been wearing one of Matt's old sweat-shirts. For once I'd found something useful about having an older brother. He'd never miss it. The sweatshirt covered me all the way to the bottom of my shorts. It was so baggy, I supposed I could wear it until the baby was born and no one would ever notice my growing figure.

I didn't want to wear any maternity clothes yet so I'd been wearing dresses every day. My friends thought I'd turned Little Miss Priss on them.

"Miss Marshall!"

From the tone of Mr. Silva's voice and all the faces turned toward me in rapt attention, I got the feeling it wasn't the first time he'd called my name.

"Miss Marshall, would you mind telling the class what is so important that you don't need to pay attention to the purpose of the judicial system?" His knuckles rapped the desk in thunderous rhythm.

I grabbed a strand of hair and pulled hard as I felt the red flow into my cheeks.

Mr. Silva knew I had no answer. His glare frightened me for the first time. "You will stay after class, Miss Marshall, and read about the judicial system during break time."

I nodded, grateful he wouldn't pry deeper.

"Heard you had a run-in with Mr. Silva," Stephanie said with laughter in her eyes as we met for lunch.

"Yeah, yeah," I said, hoping she would change the subject.

"My parents are going out tomorrow night and said I could have you over for pizza. Sound good?"

Poor Steph, still trying to be her old self. It all sounded so phony, but what better offer did I have? "Sure, I'd love to."

"Pizza's okay, isn't it?"

"Yes, Steph. Pizza's okay," I said a bit irritated.

———

My mouth watered as Stephanie opened the steaming box of pizza. Dr. Womack probably would have had a fit. All that salty meat. But who cares when your taste buds are so happy?

"I wonder if the baby will like pizza," I mused, patting the mound bulging under my dress.

"Are you going to keep it?" Steph sounded shocked.

"I suppose. What else am I going to do with it?"

"I just figured you'd give it up for adoption."

"Adoption? Give up my own flesh and blood? How selfish can you get?"

"You think that's selfish?"

"Yes. Don't you?"

She shoved another bite into her mouth, chewing before answering. "No. I think it's a very loving thing to allow your child to grow up in a family."

I laughed. "What do you think—that this child will grow up in a cage?"

I could tell she was getting frustrated. She kept shaking her hair till it almost got stuck in her pizza.

"I mean a *real* family. Father, mother, maybe a sister or brother."

"My family is plenty. Besides, I happen to like babies. They're cute and fun to cuddle. And I'll have someone to love me."

"Julie, do you really think life will be so great with a baby?" Stephanie asked as she lifted the last piece of pizza from the box.

"No, I don't think it will be great. It will be life, and life has its ups and downs. A baby will help me cope. Give me some interest in life."

Stephanie shook her head hard, tossing her hair everywhere. "Babies don't help you cope; they help you to the loony farm."

"How do *you* know?" I snapped.

She ignored the question and continued, "You can't finish school, can't go to college. You have to work, but then some sitter is raising your child for you anyway. What kind of job do you think you can get without training?"

As I sat there watching her rant and rave, I twisted beautiful ringlets into my hair.

"Oh, sure, there's welfare. I can see it forming on your lips," Stephanie went on. "But welfare is the pits, the place no one can escape from. That's not life, that's barely existence."

"Oh, quit the lecture. You've always hated kids anyway."

"I have not. I just prefer to keep them out of my life until the future. I like friends my own age, and I want to keep that interest until I get married someday and have a baby of my own."

"Well, maybe that's why you're fuming. You're jealous because I beat you to it." *What a stupid thing to say,* I yelled inside my head. *You don't even believe that garbage.*

"Ha! I'm not jealous. You weren't listening. I said, 'When I was married.' You know, have a husband?"

"Who says I won't have a husband someday?" I stuck my bottom lip out.

"Do you think men are going to flock to a girl with a ready-made family? I've seen men flatter mothers by paying attention to their children. But when the moment of truth comes, they just can't accept some other man's kid."

My eyes must have been spitting fire. "So what makes you so wise and wonderful?"

Stephanie's focus dropped to the floor. "I've been seeing Carol sometimes when she comes to visit her family."

"Carol? Since when did you become chummy with her?"

Steph flushed. "Since she started dating my brother."

"Oh," I said.

"Julie, it takes a very special man to marry someone with a child. My brother isn't even that type of guy."

"Well, what makes you think Kyle won't marry me?"

Her face turned to stone. She couldn't answer.

"Steph," I confided, "something deep inside tells me that soon Kyle will come and ask me to marry him. We'll have a small wedding and live a fun life with our baby in a cute apartment. I could take the baby on walks, pushing it all around in a stroller. We could go to the park. And when the baby gets old enough, I can push it on a swing or catch it at the bottom of a slide and—"

"And who gets up in the middle of the night with it?" Stephanie interrupted.

"I will," I said, feeling like someone slugged me in the gut.

"Don't you see, Julie? Those are just dandelion dreams."

"Dandelion dreams?"

"So beautiful, but very fragile. One puff and they're gone."

"Do you think it's impossible?" I pleaded.

"Look at the reality, Julie. Kyle doesn't love you. I don't think he ever has."

The words stabbed my already aching heart. "What do you mean by that?"

"Oh, Julie. I never wanted to tell you."

"Tell me what?" My heart sensed her next words and began to pound.

"All summer, as you gazed into Kyle's eyes, his were wandering everywhere else."

"I don't believe you." The tears began to flow. "What proof do you have?"

"Julie, Kyle asked me out at least once a week all summer. Whenever you would be in the water, skiing, he would try to get cozy with me or some other girl." Stephanie began crying as hard as I was.

"Why didn't you tell me?"

"I didn't realize you two were . . . well . . . going to bed together. I thought it wouldn't harm you not to know if you two were just friends. After all, I knew Kyle would be leaving at the end of the summer."

I threw my arms around her for support as I sobbed. Oh, how I hated Kyle, but oh, how I wanted him to come love me like he used to. Or like I thought he used to.

Now my life was ruined. How could I have been so blind? How could I let myself be used that way?

Chapter Thirteen

I woke to the dancing drumbeats of rain on the roof. I peered through half-opened eyes at the steady waterfall pouring from the eaves. Somehow the gloom comforted my broken spirit.

For several days an aching heaviness had overtaken me. I didn't know how my heart could still beat with the weight attached to it. The ache lowered my head, and each breath came with great effort. I wanted to cry, but couldn't.

Anger was the only thing that could bring tears. Then I would yell my lungs out as my pillow slammed against the wall. The picture of Kyle and me, wet and happy on his dad's ski boat, had been cut in tiny pieces and burned. The ones of us on the beach had been stomped on and thrown into the fire.

I didn't care if I ever ate again. Food tasted lousy anyway. Especially ice cream and pizza.

Zombies walked with more direction than I did. I often didn't know where I was going and didn't really care. I could have walked in front of a truck and never even seen it. If Kyle didn't care, why should I?

He'd made me feel like day-old fish, a compost

heap, or a dead cat—something that looks and smells so bad that everyone wants to hide it where they won't have to think about it anymore. So I hid myself to save them the trouble.

I rolled over in bed, struggling to get my emotions under control. I looked at my chair, sticking my tongue out at the maternity pants draped there like a limp balloon.

How could he treat me like this?

Why shouldn't he treat me like this?

I wanted him to love me. I wanted to force him to love me. Didn't he promise to love me forever? How could he have used me and then dumped me like a piece of trash? I felt like an empty candy wrapper after all the sweetness has been eaten up.

At school, I didn't care who knew I was pregnant anymore. I'd even started to wear maternity clothes.

Maternity pants are so disgusting. A square piece is cut out of the front where the zipper ought to be. In its place is stretchy fabric so your stomach can stick out as much as it wants. I hated those pants. They made me feel like a slob. I had to pull them up constantly. But what did I care? There was no one to look nice for anyway.

Just walking down the street could be a real downer. People tried to be nice, but all they did was stare at my stomach as they talked. Some didn't even try to be nice. Their noses tipped into the air.

Or they pretended not to see me. They thought they were being so clever.

I heard all the rude jokes. Ten times over. The guys at school made certain I was within hearing distance before they began.

"Hey, look at her!"

"Yeah. Didn't you hear? Now that Julie Marshall can no longer be the star volleyball player, they've asked her to be the team's official ball carrier instead!"

Their shouts of laughter echoed down the hall, and I tried not to instinctively place a hand on my "ball" stomach.

At least the girls thought my pregnancy was pretty cool. They gathered around me and wanted to touch and pat my stomach. But when it came to parties or other kinds of socializing, they didn't invite me.

With great effort, I managed to sit up in bed. Swinging my feet over the side, I tucked them into pink furry slippers. I shoved my arms into a tattered, moss-green terry robe and headed for the bathroom. Again.

Jan had been calling twice weekly for two months. I'd managed to avoid talking to her each time. But now I'd decided to go see her. Maybe she really did care. Maybe she wanted to help me. I bit my bottom lip and sucked in air. I hoped so much that she'd be the nice, caring person she'd always been. Because rejection had become part of my daily diet—and I really couldn't take any more.

Looking in the mirror, I saw a scowling prune face surrounded by wispy pieces of hair. I grabbed a comb and yanked it through the snarls. Twenty minutes later, I was sloshing through puddles—I didn't see much point in trying to avoid them—on the way to Jan's cozy house on High Street. When I got there, my feet and stomach were soaked. Dad's old tan raincoat protected the rest of me.

Jan's green eyes beamed under raised brows when she saw me. "Julie! Come in! Come in!" I felt like a long-lost relative. She even hugged me, wet coat and all. So much for the rejection theory.

Jan hung my wet coat on an antique brass hook in her entryway.

I sank into her brown plaid sofa, realizing at once I had made a mistake. *I may never be able to get out of here without the help of a crane,* I thought.

Stevie the cannonball shot out of the hallway and into my arms. Cuddling this squirming bundle that smothered me with kisses and hugs helped ease the ache in my heart. Jan sat in a brown overstuffed chair, tucking her slipper-clad feet under her.

"How's your family?" Jan asked.

"Oh," I said, gesturing with upturned palms and shrugged shoulders. "Fine, I guess."

"How are they taking your present situation?"

"I could say the family is taking this whole pregnancy bit quite well." I let the bitterness start to flow. I didn't care that it had been two months since we last spoke; she'd asked for it. "I could say Tammy is a sweet sister who is sympathetic to my aches and pains. Or that she sticks up for me when her teasing, staring friends come around. I could say Matt has stopped playing basketball and eating long enough to admit that I exist. Or I could say Dad is loving and supportive."

I stopped picking at a loose thread in her couch and turned to watch water drip from my coat onto Jan's entry floor.

Jan remained silent, her face concerned.

"I could say all that, but it would be a lie." I yanked on a strand of hair and twisted it around my finger.

"So what's the truth?" Jan asked, leaning forward to pick up Stevie.

"Tammy pretends she doesn't know me in public, laughing and staring along with everyone else. Matt pretends he doesn't know me anywhere. He just lopes around with a sandwich in his left hand, while his right hand flutters up and down, dribbling an invisible ball."

Jan laughed. "What can you expect from a 12-year-old and a first-year college jock?"

"Dad looks right through me, and I bet he

would say some pretty mean things if he talked." I pondered what he would say, tightening the grip on my hair. "I guess for once I'm glad he isn't a talker."

"What do you want from them?" Jan asked as she stroked Stevie's hair.

"I want them to accept me. I always have." I paused to stop a stray tear. "I want them to love me in spite of this." I tapped my rock-hard stomach.

Jan nodded.

"What do you think I should do about this?" I tapped it again. "I've asked everyone else."

"What do they think?"

"Most of them say I should have gotten an abortion, but since I didn't, of course, I should keep it."

"Tookie! Tookie!" Stevie chimed in. Jumping from Jan's lap, he pointed a chubby finger toward the kitchen.

"Just a minute," Jan said to both of us. She left the room, returning with a pitcher of apple juice, some cups, and animal-shaped crackers. "Want some?"

"No, thanks."

"What does your mom say?" Jan held Stevie and helped him drink his juice.

"She says if I keep the baby, I will have to move out."

Jan's brow was poised for a question.

"She says it's not that she doesn't want me to keep it. That's my decision. She feels I need to have full responsibility for it. She can't be counted on to be a live-in sitter."

"She's right."

"I guess. In off moments Tammy will tell me how she hopes I'll keep it."

"What do you want to do?"

"Oh, I don't know. I'm so confused. I suppose I should keep the baby, but I don't know if I can handle the responsibility 24 hours a day."

"Even in the best situations caring for a baby is tough."

"Not only that, but I can hardly handle myself and my emotions now."

"Pregnancy emotions are the worst roller coaster I've ever been on. What are you struggling with the most?"

"Excruciating pain. Kyle hurt me so bad. That pain and the uncertainty of the future never go away. I dream about it, feel it kicking to remind me—" I wiped at the tears as they escaped from my eyes.

Jan began to rock Stevie. "The pain will be there for a long time. It will lessen as the years pass, and someday you will realize it's gone. As for your uncertainty about the future, well . . . all I can say is I believe it would one day change into peace if you would give your problems over to Jesus and trust Him for the answer."

My jaw dropped. "You mean He would give me an answer? Straight from heaven?"

The beginnings of a smile touched the corners of Jan's mouth, and her green eyes danced. I think she would have laughed if I hadn't been so serious.

"It doesn't happen quite like that. His answers come through reading His Word, the Bible, and spending lots of time in prayer about the problem."

"So how do you know when you have the answer?"

"Most of the time I have peace. God never lets me rest until I've made the right decision. The decision still may be hard or painful. But when I follow through, I have a peace of mind and heart that I have done the best thing."

"So what do you think I should do?" I asked again. I hoped she might have an answer from God for me.

"I can't make that decision for you."

"Thanks a heap."

"Hold on. I can't make your decision, but I have a friend living in The City who counsels pregnant teenagers. Maybe you should talk to her. She might be able to help you sort it out."

So I did.

Roberta worked for the Children's Placement Society. They're an adoption agency. But Roberta surprised me. She didn't push adoption. She asked good questions. But mostly she listened.

I went to see Roberta several times. We sat in her office at the Society, a renovated Victorian house. Her window looked out over the street that dropped steeply away from us, eventually finding its end near the bay.

She always gave me a paper clip before we began to talk. She would take one, too, and we would both proceed to destroy them during each hour or two we had together.

She always wore something in a color I would never give a second glance at in a store. Bright purple or burgundy were her favorites. But she looked fabulous. The colors set off the silver in her hair. She looked like she had to be at least 50, but when she spoke, I knew she understood me.

We talked a lot about the hassles of being pregnant, about family and friends. Sometimes we even cried about Kyle. Roberta was fun and frustrating to talk to. Fun because I could tell her anything, frustrating because she made me think about this whole thing from the harder point of view—something I'd rather not have done.

Sometimes I felt as though I was in school. I mean, she gave me homework at the end of each visit. I must confess it was the most challenging and interesting homework I've ever had to do. Besides, I never got a grade and never had to turn it in. We simply talked about the results.

First, I had to shop for prices on everything

Baby would need for its first year. Clothes, diapers, food, formula, and all that kind of stuff. Then she had me break the cost down into weeks and months. Next, I had to look at housing rentals, food and clothing costs for me, then add it all up and see how the budget would work under welfare allotments or under minimum wages for a month.

I couldn't believe how much baby stuff cost. One small can of formula was over three dollars! She said you needed a couple of cans *per day* at first and about one later on.

Food was close to 40¢ a jar. One crib sheet was $9, a package of onesies was $7. Outfits were outrageous at $15 to $25! Cheap disposable diapers were $13 for 60. I guess you can go through that many in just a few days. Nightgowns, socks, bottles, blankets . . . the amount of stuff you need for a kid is staggering. And the cost even more so. Added up for a whole year—well, the total made me shudder. Yeah, there are garage sales. But just the diapers and formula cost enough to make anyone broke.

Roberta also had me write a little essay, "What Is a Parent?" That was hard. I never thought of me being a parent. Not like Mom and Dad. They're parents. I'm a kid.

Last, she had me make two lists. At the top of one sheet of paper I wrote "pros." That was where I'd write the benefits. I drew a line down the middle and labeled one side "adoption," the other "parenting." Then I wrote "cons" at the top of a second piece of paper, for the negatives. Like with the first sheet, I wrote "adoption" on one side and "parenting" on the other. After all my homework, Roberta believed I had enough information to accurately fill out the sheets.

For the next two weeks, I could think of little else. Anytime I thought of something good or bad about being a mother, I wrote it on the appropriate piece of paper. I did the same thing with adoption.

Roberta said this would help me make up my mind. Not really. It almost made my choice more difficult.

Now I didn't want to do either.

Chapter Fourteen

Fog smothered the city in a heavy, cold, damp, gray blanket. I felt I almost couldn't breathe. It even seemed to seep through the cracks around the windows.

I looked at Roberta and straightened my paper clip in one jerk. "I don't think it's possible to love the baby and give it up for adoption," I said, angry that I had to make this horrible decision at all.

Roberta raised one eyebrow, so characteristic of her when she begins to listen intently. "Why not?"

"Don't you understand?" I exclaimed. "The baby is my own flesh and blood! Give it to strangers? I can't do that!"

In her forever even-tempered voice, Roberta replied, "No girl should ever have to give her child to strangers. Intimate details of several adoptive families can be given to you so you can make your own choice as to where your child will belong. If a couple chooses to remain anonymous, you don't have to consider them." She leaned forward. "You won't know them well, but we do give you lots of information."

I tapped my finger on the arm of the chair. I

was still angry, but she had aroused my curiosity. "Like what?"

"They share their ages, hobbies, likes, dislikes, schooling, what they do for a living, their dreams for their futures, even their physical characteristics. They enclose a variety of photos. Most important, we tell the birth mother how the parents feel a child should be raised."

"Do you think these people could love an adopted child as though it were their own?"

"Yes!" Roberta said. "Because the child is *chosen* and so much effort has gone into becoming parents, most often there is great care, love, and cherishing of this child of the heart."

"Isn't it horrible to give up a child, though?"

"Adoption is the biggest gift of love a person can make."

"How can it be a gift of love?" I asked, my anger welling up inside again. I tapped the paper clip on her desk. "I think it's plain and simple selfishness. I might as well wear a banner proclaiming, 'This baby is an obstacle to my plans, so I'm getting rid of it.'"

"Look into your baby's future. What kind of life do you want the child to have? What kind of love, shelter, clothing, food, and so on?" She paused a moment, waiting for me to answer. I stared at her, bouncing my foot. "And what about you?" she reasoned. "Do you want to continue with school? Get married? What do you want your future to hold?"

Her voice, always gentle, never accusing, bore holes through my ideas.

Was it selfish not to think about what the baby's future might hold with just me, an uneducated teenager, as a mother? No father. I looked down at the scarlet carpet, drawing designs with the toe of my tennis shoe.

"So you don't think any girl should keep her baby?" I asked.

"If you are able to meet your child's needs to your satisfaction while not neglecting your own needs, then there's nothing wrong with keeping the baby." She set down her paper clip and folded her hands on the desk. "But if your needs are not being met, your child's needs won't be either." She paused a moment, then continued, "This is why adoption can be a gift of love. It can be a gift of love to yourself. You need to develop your own interests and life before you will be able to pour all you have into a child. For the child, it's a gift of love because you are making certain it will receive the physical, emotional, and material support it needs. And . . . it's a gift of love to the adoptive parents. Most have tried for many years to have their own children. Think of what it could mean to them."

"I guess all that makes sense," I relented. "But I'm sure adoption is not for me."

Roberta smiled. "Whatever your decision is, I will stand behind you and support you. But I remind you that it must be *your* decision. You are the one who must live with it for the rest of your life."

As I drove home, I thought about what she had said. I couldn't help it. Her final words stuck to me like a peanut-butter sandwich that glues itself to the roof of your mouth.

At the same time, I was tired of thinking. I felt like my brain was all wrinkled up like a used tissue. I tried to shift my attention to the road that curved and wound for miles. It was good to be out of the fog of San Francisco and to see the hills part and roll away from the road. Grapevines, pruned for the winter, had once looked like thousands of little marching men. Now they looked like a bunch of dead sticks.

I felt like a dead stick. The ache in my heart was the only thing that assured me that I was quite alive. The hole inside yawned as though it would swallow me in a very short time. I needed someone to help me. *Kyle*. I needed someone who cared about me to guide me. *Kyle*.

Nothing I told myself could persuade me to stop thinking about him. None of my pointed reminders about what a creep he'd been. None of the tapes replaying our last phone conversation. My heart's call forgave, justified, excused. *Kyle*. I wanted to call him. I *had* to call him. Maybe he felt the emptiness inside, too. Maybe he really wanted to talk to me but was afraid I'd hang up on him.

Christmas decorations still hung in each town I passed. The decorations overpowered thoughts about Kyle and reminded me of that awful, strained day. I was so glad that was over. I loved that wonderful feeling of knowing I'd ruined everyone's Christmas.

For one thing, I could tell that no one knew what to buy a pregnant girl who hadn't made a decision about her baby. I got a lot of socks and a diary. Wonderful.

Yep. Christmas had been a total bust.

Depression hung over me like a thundercloud the rest of the drive home. Once there, I helped Mom clean a bit, then sneaked up to my room. I peeked down the hall, then closed the door with extra care. The telephone shook in my hand as I dialed.

I took a deep breath. "Hello, Mrs. Browning? Is Kyle there?"

She paused a moment, probably trying to place the voice. "Oh, honey," she said in her refined manner, as though she knew perfectly well who I was. "Kyle and that cute little girl, oh, what's her name? Oh, yes—Barb—have gone out this evening. Too bad it's so chilly and foggy."

"Thank you, Mrs. Browning."

My pillow hit the wall in record time. A knock on the door invited me to join the family for Saturday night television. I refused.

As I crawled into bed, I glanced at my barren calendar. My birthday was in a week and a half. I hoped everyone would forget. I didn't need any more socks.

<hr />

I stood in front of the fireplace in Jan's living room, the palms of my hands stretched out to receive the warmth of the fire. The glow kissed my cheeks. The smell of rising bread dough made me feel like I had crawled into a warm, safe blanket.

The warmth of Jan's love surrounded me as well. I spent a lot of time at her house these days. In her presence I felt the acceptance I couldn't find anywhere else.

Jan and I sipped tea from pottery mugs, helping the fire ward off the chill filtering into our bones.

Jan sat on the floor, singing a silly song to Stevie as she changed his diaper. My thoughts began to drift again. What Roberta said had been going over and over in my mind like a stuck CD. Maybe I'd been wrong about adoption. Maybe I shouldn't have been so quick to condemn others for doing it just because it was something I couldn't do.

I rubbed my stomach where the baby kicked mercilessly.

"Where's your mind gone, Julie?"

I looked up from my reverie, shrugging my shoulders. I hadn't noticed she had quit singing.

"What are you thinking?"

I sipped some tea. "The problem of adoption is still making me crazy . . . right, wrong, selfish, loving." I shook my head. "I just don't know."

Jan pressed the tape to hold the diaper together. "The authority I rely on most speaks quite highly of adoption."

I perked up. "Really? What authority? What does it say?"

"God is my authority, and He—"

"I should have known," I interrupted, shaking my head. "Who did He ever adopt?"

"Me."

If Jan's eyes hadn't been looking directly into mine, her face radiant, I would have thought she was joking. So I toned down the sarcasm. "You *are* kidding, right?"

"I'm not kidding. He adopted me five years ago when I lived in Los Angeles." She kissed Stevie's cheek and sent him playing with his cars.

"So how does God go about adopting people?"

Jan cupped her mug of tea in her hands. "The

process is kind of like our adoptions. For example, a couple takes the first step when they want to seek a child. They pay a legal fee, papers are signed, and the child is given to the new parents for them to feed, clothe, and care for as though it was their own."

"So God went to an adoption agency, I suppose?"

Jan tipped her head back and laughed. "Hardly," she said, and sipped more tea. "That's where the difference comes in. God paid the price and has the seal all ready. But people must come to Him for that legal seal. He won't force anyone to be His child who doesn't want to be."

"Why would anyone want to be His child?"

"The benefits are so great! I feel sorry for those who prefer what little they have to what they could have as a child of God."

"What benefits?" I asked with rising curiosity.

"Mostly He gives new inner qualities: patience, gentleness, peace, kindness. He cares for our physical needs, too. There are all kinds of benefits a perfect father can bring."

"Perfect?" I felt myself sinking into a bog of hopelessness. "Oh, Jan, He wouldn't want to adopt me."

"Why not?"

"Isn't this reason enough?" I tapped my stomach. "I would be out of place as the child of a perfect father. And this is just my most obvious mistake, to say nothing of all the rest. I'm not good enough to be His adopted child."

Jan's expression softened. "No one is good enough to be a child of God. But He was willing to pay the high price for our mistakes so adoption would be possible."

I moved to sit on the braided rug with her. "But what difference will it make for me?"

"A difference in everything. In your whole life." Jan's face displayed confidence. "I now have meaning to my life. God gives me direction, constant help, and guidance. He gives me strength in weakness and peace during storms." She ignored Stevie, who ran cars over her arms and legs.

I watched him a moment, then asked, "How does someone get adopted?"

"It says in the Bible that Jesus, God's Son, is the way. We can't approach God on our own because God is perfect. Jesus paid the required legal fee through His death to make us new persons who can be at home in His family."

I tried to grasp all these things and put them in an order I understood. I sifted and filed until words and phrases made sense. It was like learning a new language.

Jan's eyes took on a different glow. "Then comes the best part. He sends a part of Himself to live inside you. Kind of like the seal put on adoption papers to make it legal. The seal is God's own

Spirit, and He will never leave you. The seal can't be altered."

I could feel the baby turning another somersault. I tried to calm the flutter in my heart.

It all came together. Hadn't I prayed that God would help, would hear? I realized that during all the time I'd known Jan, I'd started opening my heart to God. Even when I'd thought I'd slammed it shut, I was still thinking about God, letting Him pry through the cracks a little more each time. I'd ridiculed Jan because I couldn't face that she had told me the truth. But now the truth was more important than my defenses.

"Jan." My voice broke. "I want to be one of God's adopted children."

For once in my life, I had made a major decision. And there was no doubt—it was the right one.

"Okay, why don't you tell Him that?"

"Tell him? Do you mean *pray?* I don't know how to pray."

Jan cocked her head. "How do you talk to me?"

I shrugged my shoulders. "I don't know. I just do."

"That's how you talk to God," Jan said. "Just like you would talk to me."

I picked at a string from the rug. I opened my mouth and drew in a deep breath. I squeezed my eyes shut. "God," I said, then stopped. "I don't quite know what to say." I opened my eyes and looked at Jan. She gave me an encouraging smile, and I went on. "I want You to take over this mess I call my life. I want You to adopt me, change me, help me. I'm sorry I've done all sorts of dumb and wrong stuff. I want that life You promised, too, okay?"

Jan reached over and touched my hand. "Thank You, Father, for my friend Julie. I'm so glad You answered my prayers for her—that she would find You. Thanks."

I opened my eyes and looked around. Everything looked the same. I could still see and hear Stevie *vrrooom*-ing his cars around the house. I could still smell the bread. Yet something was missing. I looked down and blurted out, "It's gone!"

Jan's face furrowed with confusion. "What's gone?"

"The hole in my heart. It's finally gone." I looked at Jan, my mouth twisted into a cockeyed little smile.

Leaning over, she gave me a hug.

The phone rang, disrupting our quiet joy. "Julie, it's your mom," Jan said, handing it to me.

"Hi, Mom."

Her voice was strained. "I just thought you might like to know. Kyle's here."

Chapter Fifteen

··————··

The rain had stopped. Even the coldest January dropped little or no snow on our small town.

I put my hands in my pockets in a vain attempt to keep them warm. I tucked my head down, looking at the ground as I walked. This time I stepped around the numerous puddles—little gray mirrors flecked with bits of leaves.

I didn't want to think about home. I didn't want to think about Kyle. Yet not to think about them was an impossibility.

Why did he come? I shuddered with fear, cold, and anticipation. My heart skipped a beat. Maybe my knight had come to bear me away on his white horse.

Oh, why hadn't I worn the orchid-pink maternity top I'd splurged five nights' baby-sitting earnings on? Instead, I had worn my tattered blue thing with a grease spot in the middle of the left pocket. Tacky at best.

I slipped around to the back of the house and stepped out of my wet and muddy shoes. Countless occasions of sneaking in the house late at night had made me a pro at silently turning the back doorknob. I knew the spots in the floor that creaked and avoided them on the way to the living room.

If Kyle didn't hear my approach, he was sure to hear the pounding of my heart. I wanted to get a good, solid look at him before I had to speak. I wanted to see if memory had distorted reality.

I stopped under the stucco arch. My memory had done no justice to what I saw.

Kyle was stunning in his sapphire blue and tan rugby shirt. Blue was his best color, and he looked warm and huggable.

He was talking to my mom, his hands moving in vivid description of his latest escapades. Without even seeing them, I knew his eyes sparkled with self-confidence. It struck me as strange that he could still look Mom in the eye after all that had happened.

He was so poised, so arrogant, and so much better-looking than anyone I had ever seen. I wanted to run and throw my arms around him. At the same time, I wanted to grab the telephone and throw it at him.

Mom must have seen me from the corner of her eye. She turned her head and smiled at me. Kyle followed her gaze and turned to voice an elegant hello. I watched all pretense come crashing down around him as he stared at me. Or rather, at my stomach.

Mom slipped from the room as he tried to speak.

I should have felt bad that I enjoyed watching him flounder. I never would have believed Kyle knew what it meant to be nervous. Yet there he was, stammering. "I never . . . uh . . . never . . ."

His eyes continued to stare about two stories below my chin. This new voice was so unlike the confident smoothness I had grown used to. He tried again, his hand waving around like a confused bird. "I didn't expect you to look like . . . uh . . . this."

I wanted to ask, "What did you expect a pregnant girl to look like?" Instead, I dressed my voice with forced courtesy. "How are you?" I asked.

He again tried to look me in the eye, but there seemed to be a magnet pulling his eyes down to stare at my very round figure.

"Uh, fine. I guess." His gaze darted around the room. "My mom made me come," he blurted.

If I had hackles, they would have risen in a flash. Instead, I threw my words at him like stones. "Well, fine. You've done your duty. If you don't have anything else to say, why don't you leave?" I gritted my teeth into a rude smile. I didn't want to lose my battle with the tears beginning to form behind my eyes. His gorgeous, untouched presence suddenly made me acutely aware of my lumpy ugliness.

Part of me didn't want him to leave. Part of me wanted to pick him up and throw him through the front window.

Bewildered, he turned to leave. Halfway to the door, he stopped in his tracks. Reversing, he extended a shaking hand with a wrapped package. "Kind of a combination birthday and Christmas gift."

"Thanks," I muttered. I bet his mom chose it, bought it, and wrapped it. *Another duty*, I thought, furious.

He left without waiting for me to open the gift.

As best I could, I ran up the stairs to my room. I wanted to punch the baby for making me unable to throw myself onto the bed. Instead, I sat on a chair and sobbed.

I let the tears drop onto the pretty paper box. Golden yellow roses decorated the top. I wiped under my eyes. I tugged the end of the yellow satin ribbon. Removing the lid, I laid aside the rustling white tissue paper.

The pretty box with an assortment of colorful socks went crashing against the wall. As I watched them fall crumpled to the floor, I shouted through fresh tears, "I hate you, Kyle Browning! I hate you!"

◆━━━◆

My birthday. Over. I only received two gifts worth mentioning. The first and best was an easy-to-read-

and-understand Bible. The second was a journal.
Both were from Jan.

Soon I was getting up every day 15 minutes
early to read a paragraph or two from the Book of
John. Then I'd write what I thought about it in my
little notebook. Mostly I'd write questions.

Jan agreed to read the same thing, and then
we'd talk about what we'd found. It was fascinating.

I'd never known the Bible could actually relate
to my life, but I found that if I paid attention it
related well. The people in the Bible were real; they
just lived in a time and place I wasn't used to yet.

Anyway, the Book of John is about the life of
Jesus, and it was teaching me how He wanted me
to live. Anytime I yelled at Tammy for intruding on
my privacy or whatever, I didn't feel satisfied anymore. I felt guilty. I kept getting gentle reminders
to do better, but change isn't very easy.

I had to admit it, though—it seemed Tammy
was getting easier to live with. She didn't go out of
her way to irritate me like she used to. She even
came to me and put her hand on the baby to wait
until it moved. She always got the biggest kick out
of that. I think loving the baby was her way of also
loving me.

Even Matt was becoming civilized. He'd actually gone out of his way a few times to say hello and
a halfhearted "How are you?" For him that was
progress.

Jan said they were reacting to the change in me. I wasn't so sure. I didn't feel changed.

The best thing that had happened, though, involved Dad. He came in from work one night all grubby. He walked over to where I sat in the over-stuffed chair and pulled me out of it. It kind of scared me until I looked into his eyes.

Dad has always had the most expressive eyes. After all these months of seeing only disappoint-ment there, I now saw kindness.

His rough hands gently clasped my arms. His lips moved as if he were going to speak. I thought I saw a tear come to one eye, but he gave me no chance to make sure. He pulled me close and hugged me.

My nose tickled with wood dust as he stroked my hair once. He spoke in his brief way. "Hi, Jule."

He let go and took the stairs three at a time. Moments later I heard the shower running.

I smiled. Maybe Dad had found a way to accept me and my situation.

I loved the small changes. But it's not that my world had turned rosy. Or maybe it had—roses have thorns, you know. And I had two big ones.

The first thorn was Stephanie. As close as she and I had always been, something was splitting us apart. I tried to blame it on differing interests and figured that everything would be fine after the baby was born. We could still talk about all sorts of things, but she didn't want to socialize much more than that with me. The guy of the week had her too wrapped up. When she and I were together, she'd toss her hair and tell me about her latest fling with the latest guy she was in love with. Two weeks later that guy was a creep, and someone new had taken his place.

We still had our cinnamon rolls at break time, and we continued to eat lunch and watch the world go by. But it just wasn't the same.

One day I tried to tell Stephanie what had happened to me since I'd asked Jesus to change my life. She laughed, then sobered, admitting, "You have changed, Julie. You aren't depressing to be around anymore. It's like you have something to look forward to." Then she pouted. "It's also as if you have a special secret you can't pass on. You don't need me anymore."

"That's not true, Steph." I put down my half-eaten sandwich. "The secret is easy to pass on."

Steph waved her hand at me. "I don't need your secret. I'm doing fine on my own." She sipped her Coke. "All I really want is to be needed," she said in a dramatic voice. I figured I could thank her new acting class for that.

"I will always need your friendship, Stephanie." I knew it was true, but I suspected I wouldn't always have her friendship.

The gulf was growing too wide for either of us

to bridge the gap. Slowly we were rising to the level of social friends instead of intimate, "tell all" friends. Unless our worlds could find a spot of common ground, I was afraid all intimacy would soon be lost.

Thorn number two: What to do with the baby.

Mom bugged me a lot about this one. And she usually chose the worst times to bring it up. For example, I had a terrible case of heartburn Valentine's night when Mom thought it would be a wonderful time to discuss the future. She let herself into my room without knocking. "Have you decided what you are going to do about the baby yet?" she asked.

My pen clattered to the desk. "No. And I don't want to talk about it right now." I picked up the fallen pen and returned my attention to my English paper.

Mom smoothed her apron over her lap. I could see her plotting her next move in this little game of Baby Battle we had going.

"Don't you think," she asked with a forced smile, "that the time is coming when you need to finalize what you are going to do?"

"Yes, Mother."

She'd obviously blown that move. She sighed. "Well, let me know if I can help."

Smiling a sickeningly sweet smile, I nodded. "Of course."

She left so I could wallow alone in misery and heartburn. A bath sounded comforting. As I slipped into the hot water frosted with bubbles, I thought about my options.

No matter which way I turned, I got poked with another thorn.

One day I would see a mother with her cute little one all bundled up, its little pink face so serene and sweet as it slept—and I'd want more than anything to keep my baby. I wanted to hold it, take it to the park, and push it in the swing.

Then I'd spend time with Stevie and Jan. That's when I saw the responsibility and the hours of time involved in training a child. Or I'd listen to all the plans of the kids at school. They'd discuss colleges, careers, and dreams, and it all sounded so exciting. If I kept the baby, it would be hard to do all that. Maybe any of it.

That's when I'd start thinking maybe adoption was the best thing for me. But never to see my child again? How could I do that?

If only I could see my life one, two, three years ahead. If only I could see twenty years down the road. If only . . .

Similar thoughts kept running around and around in my head, making me dizzy with frustration. The whole thing was a relentless nightmare.

Most nights I just let my tears flow down my face. "Oh, God," I prayed. "What am I going to do? Why aren't there more choices? Why? Why? Why?"

━━━━━━

March winds blew their cold air through my clothes as though they were an open window. The clouds hung heavy and low. It would only be a matter of time before their bellies burst forth again with cold, gray rain.

My emotions were as unpredictable as the wind. Dr. Womack told me emotional upheavals were normal, along with a host of other problems: leaking breasts, my constant heartburn, stomach itching, the brown line on my abdomen, stretch marks (ugh!), and even the 24 pounds I'd gained.

I wouldn't call 24 pounds normal. I'd call it fat.

One afternoon I forced my baby-laden body up the stairs to Dr. Womack's office, cringed when the nurses weighed me, and waited to ask a very important question.

"How is everything?" Dr. Womack asked, bending over the lump on the table (me), listening to the baby's heartbeat.

"Fine, I guess."

He peered at me over the top of his glasses. "You don't sound convinced."

I shifted my weight and sat up like an awkward, rolling sea lion. "I am getting quite tired of this little bundle."

He patted my hand. "You don't have much longer to go. I still suspect your due date of April 18 is a good guess."

I let my face fall. "You mean you don't know for sure?"

He laughed. "If I could do that, I'd be a rich man. Next visit we will do an internal exam."

I wrinkled my face in disgust, twisting my hair around my finger.

Dr. Womack went on. "We'll check to see if your cervix has begun to thin out or dilate. This will give us a better idea when the baby might come."

"Dr. Womack," I said, changing the subject, "I have an important question. Why do I have to go to school?"

"You don't have to go to school. However, it's best for you to remain active. School helps with that and with the pregnancy boredom." He paused, ripples traveling up from his brows to the middle of his balding head. "I also presume you want to graduate next year?"

I nodded. Baby or no baby, I wanted to graduate. As usual, he was right. The benefits of continuing in school did outweigh the problems. At least the jokes about me had finally stopped. The kids were getting used to me and talking *to* me rather than *at* me.

It seemed, though, that everywhere I went, all eyes focused on my stomach. But you know what was the absolute worst part about school? Sitting in those uncomfortable, hard desks.

I looked up at Dr. Womack and said a half-hearted "Thanks."

He smiled. "See you in two weeks."

Chapter Sixteen

3:22 *A.M.*
    I wished the moon could talk. His face looked so wise. His lips pursed, ready to speak. He was golden as he peeked over the hills, then changed to a frosty white as he climbed higher into the sky to keep an eye on the proceedings below.

I felt as though he and I were the only ones awake. I couldn't sleep with that nagging pain in my lower back.

I never expected contractions to be like this. An incredible tightness that pushed downward had overtaken my body. It all took place inside; my outside skin wasn't even involved.

During each contraction, I could feel the entire outline of my uterus.

The pain in my back came at the same time as the contractions in the front. Both pains together made me real uncomfortable. Walking around made me feel much better. I guess it gave me a false sense of accomplishing something.

If I could have sat still long enough, I'd have written in my diary. I knew exactly what I'd have said:

April 24. My body has begun to churn and creak and groan. I am going to have a baby, and it will probably be today. Will I be able to make a wise decision about its future? The baby has been with me so long. I know its every move. We are a part of each other. It can't leave me now.

When I last spoke with Roberta 10 days ago, she seemed matter-of-fact when I told her I found it impossible to make a decision. She told me I needn't decide anything final until after the baby was born. I did choose a family, though. Just in case. They loved the outdoors, pets, children, and had an excellent education. He was an engineer, and she was a teacher. Best of all, both had Jesus as a friend, just like I did.

———

I caught my breath as another contraction began tightening its grip on me. I realized I'd been denying the baby's existence even until that day. Then the truth overwhelmed me. Involuntarily, I shivered.

I was very, very scared.

6:00 A.M.

The contractions were so hard that I had to stop and either sit down or bend over when one hit. It was impossible to walk during a contraction. I expected Mom to be up any minute to get ready for work. I hated to intrude on her life with my messy business. Why couldn't I have had the baby on a weekend so it would be more convenient for everyone?

10:00 A.M.

The white hospital walls were bare except for a huge black-and-white clock. I got to stare at it while I sat in bed. I could watch the second hand slow down during each contraction.

The nurse had shown me how to take deep breaths during a contraction. The pain wasn't so severe and the breathing exercises helped me relax a bit.

Mom sat beside me, staring blankly at the television. She jumped to life each time I began to moan with another contraction.

It was going to be a long day. Dr. Womack had already come in to check me. He predicted the baby would come sometime in the evening. I didn't think I could survive that long. But I was only dilated three centimeters. That meant, he said, the opening in the uterus, where the baby must come out, had opened to about three fingers' width. It had to open to ten centimeters before the baby could fit through.

11:00 A.M.

A plump nurse wearing a lavender uniform walked in carrying a small tray. "Hi," she said sweetly. "I'm going to prep you now."

I looked at my mother, then back to the nurse. "What do you have to do?"

She filled a small bowl with warm water from the sink, looking over her shoulder as she spoke. "It isn't painful. We shave a small area of your pubic hair. Just around the vaginal opening."

I flinched, scrunching my face.

The nurse noticed my intense displeasure and smiled. "Be glad we don't give enemas anymore."

I gulped.

She finished in a flash, and allowed me to go to the bathroom.

I lowered myself onto the toilet, using the handrails on each side. Thankfully, she closed the door, allowing me some dignity.

I was okay until a contraction came. My moaning brought both my mother and the nurse running. They opened the door, and I motioned them away.

Five minutes later I came out, bent like an old lady checking out her garden.

12:00 noon

They offered to bring my Mom some lunch. "Oh, yes, please," I told them. "I'm starving."

The nurse handed me a cup of ice chips. "Here's your lunch. If you eat, you might vomit later when the contractions get harder."

Harder? I thought they were hard enough already. I just loved her blunt way of saying things.

I was now dilated to five centimeters. Halfway there.

2:00 P.M.

I detested not being in control of myself. But now I was at the mercy of another force.

The contractions felt like ocean waves. The power gathered, sucking and pulling, and building to a peaking grip of pain. Suddenly it would subside, losing strength until all relaxed.

A few minutes would pass, then another wave. Each contraction was stronger than the last. With each one I gripped the handrails, trying not to cry out.

I looked into my mother's eyes, imploring her to help. Her eyes returned a look of understanding, of love, of remembrance.

The nurse came in through the haze of pain, offering a shot of Nubain to ease the force. I turned her down, not wanting to lose the control I had left.

The next contraction brought a release of pressure and an abundance of wet warmth.

"Mom, get the nurse, quick."

Without hesitating, Mom ran and brought back a nurse.

"What's happening?" I pleaded.

The nurse took one look at the large blue pad protecting the bed and smiled. "The water sac that surrounds the baby has ruptured. Your contractions should go a little faster and harder now."

She quickly changed the pad to a dry one and bustled out the door.

3:00 P.M.

The nurses on the new shift came in one at a time to check on me. One offered Nubain. I agreed this time.

I was now dilated to seven centimeters. I almost didn't care.

4:30 P.M.

The way Mom stared at me gave me the creeps. I wished she'd leave.

Dr. Womack came to check on me again. He was smart to avoid dumb questions like, "How are you?" or "How's it going?" He didn't stay long. Just long enough to tell me I was in transition. Whatever that meant.

I'd grown tired of all this. I wanted to go home and maybe come back to finish this later. Then again, maybe not.

Mom left to get a Coke. I hoped she would hurry back.

6:00 P.M.

I was sitting on the toilet, holding on to the rails beside it as though they were the only things keeping me from falling in.

My body uncontrollably folded in half, bearing down as though I had to expel something.

The nurse pounded on the door. "Are you okay, Julie?"

I could barely talk. "Yeah. I feel like I'm constipated. That's all."

"Come out. *Now*. That feeling is the baby coming down the birth canal."

I pulled myself up using the rails. I couldn't have gotten up without them. The nurse opened the door and helped me to bed.

"Lie back and relax," she said. "I'm going to do a manual exam to check you again."

I groaned but obeyed. I didn't feel like arguing.

Her gentle hands probed as she spoke. "Yes, the baby's head is beginning to protrude through the cervical opening. Next time you have a contraction, I want you to push with all your might."

She showed me how to pull myself up by my knees and bear down as hard as I could, holding my breath.

7:05 P.M.

Two nurses dressed in blue scrubs entered the room.

One positioned herself at the head of my bed, the other at the foot. The one at the foot of the bed spoke. "Okay, Julie. The baby's head is crowning. I can see it at the entrance to your vagina. It is time to go to Delivery."

She and the other nurse pushed the bed through the doorway and down the hall. Under normal circumstances, I would have been embarrassed at even this short jaunt, considering I was wearing practically nothing. At that moment, though, I couldn't have cared less.

They wheeled me into a brightly lit room. All around were contraptions with cords and tubes hanging on them. In the corner was a small bed. Clear plastic sides revealed a tiny mattress and sheets.

The delivery table was in the center of the room. It looked almost identical to the doctor's exam table, only larger.

The nurses helped me to get onto it. It wasn't an easy task. Because of the baby in the birth canal, I couldn't bend.

I had the distinct feeling the baby would come out at any moment, but they didn't seem to be the least bit worried.

Dr. Womack appeared, eyes crinkled in a smile. A mask covered the rest of his jolly face. "Hello again, Julie. Let's get to work so we can meet this baby!"

I just looked at him, panting with fright and pain. My head felt light and heavy at the same time.

Dr. Womack patted my leg. "It's okay, Julie. You're doing just fine."

A mirror, placed just beyond my left foot, reflected a distorted image of my lower body. I could see the baby's head forcing its way out.

Dr. Womack gave me an injection right next to the baby's head. "This will numb you so I can make a small incision. The size of the baby's head indicates your skin might tear if we don't."

I felt much stretching, pressure, and a strong

movement as the baby's head came out with the next contraction.

"Just one more push," Dr. Womack encouraged, "and we'll have the rest of the baby out, too."

It took three pushes and the baby came sliding out. I panted and cried with relief. I tried to peer down at the little, slimy, pink-and-purple thing covered with white cornstarch—the thing they claimed to be my baby.

A small cry filled the room as it sucked in its first breath of air. I looked at my baby in wonder.

"It's a boy."

My whole mind could have been blown away with a feather. How could that living being have come from inside me? I wanted to touch him, to hold him.

The nurse wrapped him up in a warm towel and laid him in my arms. I suddenly felt timid and awkward holding this little warm bundle of baby. I thought about Roberta and the family hoping and waiting for him. Yet . . . how could I give away this little wonder?

A piece of my heart bloomed at that moment. A brand new piece I'd never been aware of before. It bloomed with overpowering love for this little guy. I felt I knew him. His little black eyes stared into mine, seeming to know who I was, too. I wanted to love him in every way I could.

In that second I changed. My love for this little

guy grew me up. I understood now the power of giving birth. I understood that I would never go back to being the Julie I'd been hours before.

Whatever happened, I knew he and I shared a bond that nothing and no one could break.

Then my arms started to shake from fatigue. "Nurse," I asked, "can you take him?" I felt bad that I couldn't hold him anymore, but exhaustion and fear came over me, and I was afraid I might drop him. I looked into the nurse's eyes. "Can someone go tell Mom?"

She nodded. "Someone already has."

I felt the doctor pushing on my suddenly flat, Jell-O-like stomach. "The placenta will be out in a moment," he announced.

I hadn't thought of that. After nourishing the baby for nine months, its job was done. It came out purple, red, blue, and white—a many-colored jellyfish.

Dr. Womack sewed up the incision he had made to allow for the baby's head. When he finished, he took off his gloves and clasped my hand between his two strong ones. "You've done good, Julie." He winked and gave my hand a final squeeze before he sailed out the door.

The transfer back to my rolling bed was a breeze. A quiet nurse wheeled me to a private room. I was grateful to whoever had the sensitivity to my situation. I needed to be alone.

Aside from being so tired I could have slept a week, I thought I might starve. Finally a volunteer brought a tray of delicious food, but when I began to eat, my appetite fled.

Mom came in to smile and stare. I stopped my picky eating and declared, with my fork waving for emphasis, "I don't want any visitors except Jan."

Mom looked disappointed. "Not even Dad or Stephanie?"

"No, Mom. No one." I turned my head away as my eyes filled with tears. "I have too much to think about." Besides, I didn't want the world to prance through to stare at me, the sideshow freak.

When morning came, I begged to see my little boy again. My son. The day before seemed unreal until I touched him again.

As I held him, caressing that little face and checking out that little body, a battle of feelings overwhelmed me.

How could I reasonably give this child a stable home life when I was nowhere near knowing what I was going to do with my life next week, much less next year or five years from now? To add a little life to that confusion didn't seem fair—to either of us.

But on the other hand, this little guy was so much a part of me. Just by touch I knew he was mine, even though he didn't look a bit like me.

He really didn't. He looked like a little fuzzball. His hair was so pale it could hardly be seen, and it was so sparse you would have thought you were touching an oversized peach, not a baby's head.

I wanted to take him home and cuddle him forever. At the same time, I secretly hoped someone would come cuddle me.

I talked to him softly, letting my hair fall in front and almost touch the baby. "Do you know that I love you? Do you know that I want what's best for you? Would you know that if I stepped out of your life so you could have two parents who love you, too?"

Tears dripped onto the baby.

"God, what am I going to do? What do You want me to do?" For once I really wanted His answer.

My spirit whispered prayer after prayer. After a while, the tormenting confusion left, and I knew the best answer. At least for that day.

Roberta had spoken of foster care. A foster family could take care of the baby until I made my final decision. That way I wouldn't have to make a lifetime choice that day.

I buzzed the nurse. She took the baby, then returned with release papers. The papers said the adoption agency could take the baby from the hospital and place him in foster care for a few days.

Jan appeared about ten-fifteen. "I just saw him, Julie. He's beautiful. I hate to say this, but he is far prettier than Stevie was."

"Thanks."

"Here, open this." Jan handed me a package wrapped in paper decorated with rainbows.

I hesitated. *Please*, I thought, *no more socks*. I opened it slowly. A smile caught my mouth, and my heart warmed. I lifted out a beautiful, pink, silky nightgown and robe to match. "Oh, Jan."

She just smiled, her green eyes twinkling.

"Thank you so much." I leaned over and gave her one of my rare hugs.

"What are you going to do, Julie?"

"Oh, Jan." I began to cry. "I don't know. I just don't know."

Chapter Seventeen

M y bowl of Crisp Crunchies were no longer crisp, nor did they crunch. Soggy lumps, like swollen maggots, lay there in a milky sea. No longer did they dance with anticipation.

Dumping the mess into the sink, I got a dry bowl and started over. I wanted to eat before Stephanie arrived.

Perhaps today no one would call and try to gossip with my mother about the subject of the year: me. Most people didn't know Mom went back to work yesterday. So they continued calling to discuss my situation with her.

I could feel their embarrassment trickle through the phone as they attempted to cover their awkwardness about speaking with me. Their voices flickered with nervousness as they talked about inane things like the weather or their dog. You'd think I'd never had a baby.

When I came home from the hospital, I thought things would have changed. I don't know what I expected to be different. The furniture hadn't been moved. We sat at the same places to eat dinner. My room was just as I had left it, except the bed had clean sheets. My diary still lay open to where I'd tried to write about labor.

Everyone came and went at the same times. All was the same.

But all was different.

Yes, I'd grown up. Too fast, for sure. I wished I could have stayed a kid for my allotted time. But no such luck.

I knew it was going to be hard to return to school in the fall. My experiences had left me feeling awkward and out of place among my friends. Their gossip and arguments didn't interest me anymore. But I was jealous of them, and of Matt and Tammy. They had retained their innocence.

Every time I saw Tammy she would turn her head and walk the other direction. She was angry with me for not bringing the baby home. She wanted to hold him, baby-sit him, and change his diapers. She thought I'd deserted him.

I overheard Matt and Tammy talking about me the day I got home from the hospital. I was about to leave my room when I heard their voices muffled in the hall.

"It's a good thing," I heard Matt say. "I wouldn't want a screaming baby around while I try to study."

I didn't wait to hear Tammy's answer. I turned and flung myself onto the bed and sobbed into my pillow.

Tension as thick and tough as a cheap steak filled our house for the remainder of the week.

Dad didn't know how to handle me, either. His conversation was limited to "How are you feeling?" After asking that 10 times, I think he decided I would always say, "Fine." Then the conversation would promptly stagnate, and he would revert to silence and look the other way.

Mom, on the other hand, kept up a constant chatter about nothing. She tried to have something for me to do all the time. I never got a chance to think.

This week was going better. The family had stopped treating me like a fragile egg. Physically I was feeling better, too. The milk in my breasts was about dry, so they weren't full and heavy anymore and had stopped leaking. Too bad they couldn't stay that size. I'd have liked that a lot.

I couldn't get into my regular clothes yet. My stomach had lost all muscle tone. Extra skin rippled around me like Jell-O. I desperately hoped that would go away.

I finished my bowl of cereal as the doorbell rang.

Stephanie had ditched school to come see me. I had spoken to her last night for the first time since the baby was born. Before that, I could hardly talk to anyone without crying or falling asleep. Having a baby sure does weird things to your system.

I opened the door to see her eyes sparkle and dance with the excitement of seeing me. But her excitement turned to dismay when she saw my stomach. It still looked five months pregnant and must have shocked her.

"It'll go away," I assured her.

Relieved and rolling her eyes, she exclaimed, "Good." She bounced into the house, making herself at home on the sofa. "So," she said with a toss of her hair. "Tell me all about it."

I have never seen someone so curious that they couldn't sit still. She bounced her crossed leg and rubbed her hands in anticipation.

"All about what?" I teased.

"All about the birth," she replied, impatient. "I want to know every little detail."

So I embarked on the journey, starting with the backaches. Whenever she sensed I had left something out, she probed until I returned an answer more suitable to her liking. We chatted like two little old ladies who exchanged the latest gossip heard at the beauty shop.

When I finished my story, you would have thought someone we were talking about had entered the room. Our conversation stopped dead, and we suddenly had nothing more to say.

"I'd better go now," said Stephanie in her soft, awkward voice. "Let me know when you feel up to a movie or something."

I figured she only offered out of courtesy. We said the polite good-byes of two strangers. I watched her walk to her bike, swing her leg over the seat, and take off in the direction of school. As I watched her pedal away, it reminded me again of the hot day when I met Kyle.

I hadn't seen him in over three months. It bothered me when I thought of how I treated him that day. I had held back all the patience and kindness God had just given me. I guess I hadn't realized I had enough to share.

It was weird to think Kyle didn't even know he was the father of a seven-and-a-half-pound boy. Kyle, a father. Just saying it sounded ridiculous. In truth, I could never picture Kyle as a father.

But he did have rights to the baby. The adoption agency had said they would call me as soon as they had contacted him regarding the adoption. I'd told them I wouldn't make my final decision until I knew whether Kyle would sign relinquishment papers.

It was so hard to wait.

Chapter Eighteen

The phone rang over and over. It stopped before the machine picked it up. The song that had sent me rushing into the past had long since ended. I glanced at the clock. Two hours had passed.

I was glad I had been alone. It was good to cry and think without anybody barging in. With a heavy sigh, I finished folding the clothes for Mom and placed them on her bed.

The phone began to ring again. I took a deep breath and headed for my room. I sat on the bed and picked up the phone.

Roberta's voice sounded as matter-of-fact as always. "We've reached Kyle."

"Oh." I tried to remain calm as my heart leapt in my chest.

"He signed the papers."

I was afraid to ask. "Which ones?" My heart felt like a caged tiger, beating itself against the bars confining it.

Roberta paused. "The waiver."

I caught my breath. His choice to sign Denial of Paternity would have been less of a blow than this. To me, the waiver declared, "I don't care. I don't care about the baby, I don't care about Julie. I don't care."

The words of the waiver danced through my mind:

I do hereby waive my right to further notice of adoption planning of said child. It is fully understood by me that with the signing of this document I give up any further rights to said child.

Roberta interrupted my thoughts. "Have you made your final decision?"

"Yes," I said with determination. My last hope of Kyle's love was gone with the dash of a pen. *Oh, God*, I felt my heart cry, *please take care of my little boy.* Aloud I said, "I love him, Roberta. But he needs a family."

I tried to listen to her instructions through a pain-clouded mind.

"We will meet at Wohlford's Family Restaurant in Santa Rosa. Ten o'clock tomorrow morning. Okay?"

I stifled a sob. "Yes."

I hung up. I let sobs overtake me. I'd tried to pretend the adoption didn't make me sad. I'd been angry at the world for allowing this to happen to girls like me. I'd been depressed enough to fill two psychiatric hospitals. I'd even felt no one loved me or cared about this.

Mostly, I'd come to realize all of my feelings were okay. It was okay to cry. It was okay to feel empty. And it was okay to feel peace that I'd done the right thing.

"———"

The sun hurt my eyes. I wore sunglasses to hide the red, swollen lids. I strode quickly, head down, to Jan's house.

Jan cried with me. Then we prayed. As always, I felt a new strength to face my world at home.

I'd need that strength more than ever. At dinner I planned to announce my decision.

Chapter Nineteen

❖ ━━━━━━━━ ❖

I watched the clock by the side of my bed, calculating each minute as it ticked by. Each minute winged my little boy farther from me and closer to his new parents.

I could picture them as they drove to the airport. They would get there far too early. Eager, so eager, they would pace the airport, hand in sweaty hand. They'd stop to buy a sweet roll and coffee and find they could not eat or drink.

They would stand by the tinted windows, watching each plane as it arrived. An eternity of minutes would pass until the plane pulled up to the arm that reaches out to gather the passengers into the terminal.

With hearts in their throats, they'd move without speaking to the fenced-off area into which they are not allowed. They would wait. They would search the arms of every woman passenger. They would search for the flash of lavender indicating Roberta had arrived.

They would begin to lose hope as the stream of passengers dwindled to a trickle of stragglers. Their hands would clutch as a woman approached. In her arms would be a bundle with only a fuzzy fair head peeking out of the soft blanket.

The woman would speak. "Are you Mrs. Booth?"

Roberta would nod. "And you?"

The man, tall and fair-headed, would speak hesitantly, introducing himself and his wife to Roberta.

Smiling, Roberta would say, "I think I have something that belongs to you."

With that, both would begin to cry. I could imagine how anxious the woman would be to touch this little one she had waited and prayed for, for so long.

Roberta would wisely instruct them to sit, and she would place my little boy into their eager arms. They'd coo and cry over him as if they had birthed him themselves.

They'd sign the remaining papers without pausing to read them and then change him into the blue outfit they had brought for him. Roberta would leave to catch her return plane.

The couple would sit for a while longer, unable to get up. They would fear that if they did, their dream might burst. But then the baby would start to cry, and they would head to the car where they would feed him.

I could imagine the man driving more cautiously

than he ever had before. He was taking the three of them home, to *their* home.

Oh, God. My heart wanted to break.

———

The minutes tick off portions of my life. Not one can ever be retrieved.

Nothing about my past can be changed. The choices I've made will affect me forever.

My future will be different because I'm a different person than when I met Kyle. I'm not desperate for love and acceptance anymore.

Sometimes I don't feel loved, yet I know I am. God loves me. And He promises that my present and my future are in His careful, loving hands.

Sometimes that promise is all I have to keep me going.

FOCUS ON THE FAMILY®

Welcome to the Family!

Whether you received this book as a gift, borrowed it, or purchased it yourself, we're glad you read it. It's just one of the many helpful, insightful, and encouraging resources produced by Focus on the Family.

In fact, that's what Focus on the Family is all about — providing inspiration, information, and biblically based advice to people in all stages of life.

It began in 1977 with the vision of one man, Dr. James Dobson, a licensed psychologist and author of 18 best-selling books on marriage, parenting, and family. Alarmed by the societal, political, and economic pressures that were threatening the existence of the American family, Dr. Dobson founded Focus on the Family with one employee and a once-a-week radio broadcast aired on only 36 stations.

Now an international organization, the ministry is dedicated to preserving Judeo-Christian values and strengthening and encouraging families through the life-changing message of Jesus Christ. Focus ministries reach families worldwide through 10 separate radio broadcasts, two television news features, 13 publications, 18 Web sites, and a steady series of books and award-winning films and videos for people of all ages and interests.

• • •

For more information about the ministry, or if we can be of help to your family, simply write to Focus on the Family, Colorado Springs, CO 80995 or call (800) A-FAMILY (232-6459). Friends in Canada may write Focus on the Family, PO Box 9800, Stn Terminal, Vancouver, BC V6B 4G3 or call (800) 661-9800. Visit our Web site — www.family.org — to learn more about Focus on the Family or to find out if there is an associate office in your country.

We'd love to hear from you!

Devotions Designed
With You in Mind

Want More? Life
Go from ordinary to extraordinary!
Want More? Life will help you
open the door to God's abundant life.
You'll go deeper, wider and higher in
your walk with God in the midst of
everyday challenges like self-image,
guys, friendships and big decisions. Paper
back.

Want More? Love
You may ask, "Does God really
love me? How can He love me —
with all my faults and flaws?"
Want More? Love is a powerful
devotional that shows you how
passionately and protectively
God loves and cares for you — and
how you can love Him in return!
Paperback.

. . .

What You Want to Know But Were Afraid to Ask

Bloom: A Girl's Guide to Growing Up

You have lots of questions about life. *In Bloom: A Girl's Guide to Growing Up*, your questions are addressed and answered with the honesty teens expect and demand. From changing bodies, to dating and sex, to relationships, money and more, girls will find the answers they need. Paperback.

"This is a must-read for EVERY young woman!"
— Joe White, Director of Kanakuk Camps

"I grew up reading Brio *magazine (and actually still do)! Now they've written a book about what it means to be a teen and how to become a beautiful woman in God's eyes. Enjoy reading, girls!"*
— Tricia Brock, Superchic[k]

• • •

Look for these special books in your Christian bookstore or request a copy by calling (800) A-FAMILY (232-6459). Friends in Canada may write Focus on the Family, PO Box 9800, Stn Terminal, Vancouver, BC V6B 4G3 or call (800) 661-9800.

Visit our Web site (www.family.org) to learn more about the ministry or find out if there is a Focus on the Family office in your country.

Faith Made Fun

Brio Magazine
It's the inside scoop—for girls
from 12 to 16—with hot tips on
everything from fashion and
fitness to real-life faith.

Every issue of Brio has:
- Inspiring articles about Christians in
  the news — entertainers, athletes and even missionaries.
- Lots of real-life stories of ordinary girls
  doing extraordinary things
- Tips on fashion, food and friendship
- Everyday ways to set a good example
- Encouraging advice to ignite your faith
- Humor, fiction and a doctor's column
- Answers to questions about music and movies

And Don't Forget!
- Boys. Fitting in. Parents. School. Life.

• • •

Request a copy of *Brio* magazine by
calling (800) A-FAMILY (232-6459). Friends in Canada
may write Focus on the Family, PO Box 9800, Stn Terminal,
Vancouver, BC V6B 4G3 or call (800) 661-9800.

Visit our Web site (www.family.org) to learn more about the ministry
or find out if there is a Focus on the Family office in your country.